worldwide crush

worldwide crush

A Novel

KRISTIN NILSEN

SPARKPRESS

Published by SparkPress, a BookSparks imprint,
A division of SparkPoint Studio, LLC
Phoenix, Arizona, USA, 85007
www.gosparkpress.com

Published 2023
Printed in the United States of America
Print ISBN: 978-1-68463-192-6
E-ISBN: 978-1-68463-193-3
Library of Congress Control Number: 2022921783

Interior design by Tabitha Lahr

To all the boys I've loved before: Shaun Cassidy, Andy Gibb, Davy Jones, David Cassidy, Parker Stevenson, all the Bee Gees, and a fourteen-year-old Justin Bieber who made me remember it all.

And to Annie, who said, "Do it anyway . . ."

(cue music)

I travel the world to find you.
I'm searching for your face in the crowd.
Is it you who's gonna make me feel alright?
Is it you?
Is it you?

Won't you look into my eyes?
Please find me.
Please find me.

Won't you help me realize that you'll find me,
you'll find me?
I can feel it in my heart that you're out there . . .
You're my crush (my crush, my crush),
My worldwide crush.

—from "Worldwide Crush"
   Music and lyrics by Rory Calhoun

chapter 1

I love Rory Calhoun.

I've loved him forever.

Since before summer, even.

The first time I saw him was a concert in Paris. Or maybe it was Venice? Or Rome or something? Whatever, I'm not sure, the important thing is that I felt a prickly, melty warming in my stomach. It was not something I had ever felt before. And I liked it.

I was at Shauna's house, and she opened her laptop, and she said, "Watch this." It was a clip of him singing "Worldwide Crush" at a concert in Paris or Venice or whatever. And it only took a few seconds for me to understand why all those girls were huddled below him, reaching out, wishing for just a quick swipe of his hand, just a taste of his skin, which would be the most important thing to ever happen to them. And then when he put his hand on his heart and smiled—his teeth are *so* straight!—saying, "*Ti amo! Ti amo!*" it felt like he was telling *me* that he loved me. Oh yeah, *ti amo* is Italian for "I love you," so it must have been Venice. Or Rome. Anyway . . . that was an important day for me.

Now I stare at the poster on my closet door, the big one I bought with my own money, where he's squinting in the sun, his shiny blondish hair tousled by what I imagine are ocean breezes. I don't know how long I've been staring at it—a long time, I think. And when I close my eyes, I can actually see Rory and me together after his concert, holding hands as we run to his tour bus. And he would look at me and say, "How was it? Did I do okay?"

"Oh, Rory," I'd say, running my hands through my luscious, unusually smooth hair. "You were awesome. You can't even be unawesome."

Yes, I know, that's a really dumb response, but this particular fantasy is a work in progress. I'm working on it, I promise.

And then he would smile and throw his head back like "whew!" and pull me to him and wrap his arms around me and nuzzle his face into my neck and whisper, "Thanks for being with me . . ."

It could happen . . . right?

"Millie!"

My mom screams for me, ruining a perfectly good daydream. Millie is short for Millicent—barf. It's like I'm a nurse from World War II or something. Why couldn't my parents pick a nice new name from the twenty-first century?

"*Millie!*"

"What?!" I say. "*What?!*" Why does everyone want me all the time?

The voice comes up the stairs like a bullet train. "Are you all packed for tomorrow?"

"Yes!" I yell back.

"Then what's that?" Jeez Louise! My mom magically appears in my doorway and points to a shopping bag full of school supplies under my desk.

"Except that. I just need to pack that."

She's still in her scrubs from work, even though she got home like three hours ago. All night, there's been a lot of stomping and sighing and opening and closing of drawers and pointing out things that I haven't done. It's like she's the one who's stressed, even though I'm the one starting school tomorrow.

"Do you have a lunch packed?"

"Um . . . I don't know if I'm supposed to bring a lunch this year. I think I'm supposed to buy a school lunch."

My mom leans on my doorframe, just inches from my Rory Calhoun poster, with her hand on her hip, narrowing her eyes at me, like she thinks I'm bluffing. This year, we seventh graders will be eating with the eighth graders, the top dogs at Susan B. Anthony. Carrying an insulated lunch tote suddenly feels awkward for me, like my mommy packed it with a special graham cracker treat or something. I've been practicing in front of my bedroom mirror, and I just can't find a way to pull it off successfully.

"Why do you think you're 'supposed' to buy a lunch?" my mom asks. "They can't require you to buy a lunch."

"I don't know. I think I just heard that. On the bus last year."

"Yes, the bus." She starts scrubbing at a ten-year-old crayon mark on my wall. "I forget what a reliable source of information that can be." She says this under her breath, like she thinks I can't hear, even though I'm sitting on my bed, right in front her. "Fine, whatever," she says. "Just don't forget to get some cash from me in the morning." Then she bends over and starts picking up laundry off the floor like she's running out of time, like there's a deadline for the laundry. "Sweetheart, can you do me a favor and help Billy pack his backpack?"

Yes, we are Millie and Billy. You can't see me, but I'm rolling my eyes right now because I'm so annoyed and embarrassed by that blunder in parenting. When my brother was born, my parents named him Wilhelm, but by the time they got home from the hospital, they were calling him Billy. And even though I was just a little kid, like seven years old, I was like, "Hey, you guys, that is not okay."

"Mom, I was in the middle of something."

"It looked to me like you were lying on your bed, staring at the ceiling."

"How do you know that wasn't something? Why can't that be something?"

"Well, if that's something, then I'm doing it wrong. Please, just help him, so we can all get to bed before midnight."

"What's midnight?" Billy's voice comes out of my closet. How long has he been in there?!

My mom opens my closet door, and there he is. He has a ring of chocolate around his mouth. My face burns at the thought of him curled up behind the poster I was just daydreaming to.

"What's on your mouth?" my mom says to him.

"What do you mean?" One of my sleeves from a hanging shirt rests on top of his head.

"You have chocolate all over your mouth."

"No, I don't." He swipes the back of his hand across his mouth as if we're not right there watching him do it. Then he puts his hand in his pocket, which tells me he has chocolate chips in there. That's great. He's been eating half-melted chocolate chips on the floor of my closet.

My mom turns to me and mouths the words "Help me . . ."

So I slowly peel myself off my comfy bed, and she takes her armful of emergency laundry out my bedroom door and down the stairs to perform an emergency laundry operation.

Billy is little, just turned five, and starting kindergarten tomorrow. He has these big blue eyes that look like baby doll eyes with thick black lashes. When he's excited, he opens them very wide, like perfect circles. And when he's sad, they change shape ever so slightly, making him look like a sad baby deer. It breaks your heart, and then you're like, "It's okay! It's okay! Do you want some candy?" Anything so you don't have to witness such crushing sadness.

He also likes to wear a Darth Vader mask and sniff a travel-size men's deodorant.

"Millie, which state has the most tar?"

And he likes to ask unanswerable questions.

"I'm not sure, Billy. Why don't we go find your backpack?" I walk him down the hall toward his room, holding his hand so he doesn't get distracted by the wedding photo—the one where my mom has curly hair, and my dad has a goatee—on the wall by the bathroom. He stares at that photo every day, trying to make sense of it, like he knows who it's supposed to be but doesn't believe it.

He stops to look, but I tug on his hand and keep moving toward his bedroom. I find his backpack in a plastic crate and look on his desk for newly purchased school supplies. He's preoccupied, opening and closing his mouth.

"Millie, when you open your mouth, does your chin go down, or does your head go up?"

"I don't know . . . Try it slowly, and let me know what you find out. Is this your pencil box?" I can't tell if he's nodding his head or just opening and closing his mouth for research purposes.

"Millie . . ." His eyes change shape just a little bit, like a sad baby deer. "Can I bring my deodorant to school tomorrow?" He takes the cap off and holds it under his nose, looking at me.

"I suppose. Why? Are you nervous?" I give him a concerned-big-sister look.

"I don't know." He gives it another sniff and then turns around and walks out the door, right past the wedding photo, without stopping. I hear my closet door open . . . and close. I swear to G-o-d, what is so great about my closet?

Later that night, I open my underwear drawer and find my green notebook with the letters "RC" erased into the cover. Did you know you can erase the color from a standard school notebook cover with a pencil eraser? True story. My RC notebook is for documentation and data collection. I record and collect information, or "data" as my mom calls it—"What does the data tell us, Millie?"—about Rory Calhoun. You know, stuff I see online or hear on the radio. Or I'll write down comments about his newest video or an interview he did on TV. And sometimes I write letters to him. Well, not *to him*, to him, because I don't actually send them. They're more like thoughts I share with him in my notebook in a *theoretical* sense—like if he *theoretically* read my notebook after I *theoretically* left it on my stadium seat after I *theoretically* went to his concert. It just seems like something a number one fan should do.

And I say "number one fan" with finger quotes around it, because I'm not like a stalker fan. I don't want to take the guy hostage or anything; I just want to love him. And I *wish* he could love me back. I also know that Rory has gobs and gobs of number one fans, like for instance, everyone I know. But I watch these number one fans, and I don't think any of them have the same sort of feelings for him that I do. At lunch one time, my friend Shauna rolled up my *TeenTalk* magazine and thwacked a dumb boy on the head when he asked if her grandma had picked out her clothes that day (she had). I think I am the last person on earth to get a paper magazine in the mail, by the way—but where else would I get all these posters? Then Shauna just stuffed the rolled-up magazine in my backpack as if Rory Calhoun's face wasn't getting all smushed and mangled. Sweet Cheez-Its, I just couldn't take it. People my age have no idea what to do with magazines; they think they're junk mail or something.

So despite the fact that everyone loves him (like *luvs* him), I'm the one who really knows what he's like as a person. I know more than just his eye color (blue) and his signature color (aquamarine) and his shoe size (9) and that my heart tightens a little bit every time he sweeps his bangs out of his eyes. My notebook research tells me he wants to buy his mom a Mini Cooper, and his pet peeve is lying, and he went to Mill Street School, and his favorite subject was music (duh). And his dog, Sgt. Pepper, died this summer, and they had a funeral for him in his grandma's backyard, and he's worried he'll never have another dog he loves so much, and all he wants for Christmas is to be at home with his mom and his grandma and maybe get some Funyuns in his stocking.

This is why I love him. In addition to the blue eyes and the honey-blond hair and the amazing teeth, the data tells me that Rory Calhoun is a real and lovable person. And my mom says data doesn't lie.

I open my notebook and write:

Dear RC,

First day of seventh grade tomorrow. I hope Shauna and I get our regular seat on the bus. I hope my hair behaves. I hope I'm not alone in any of my classes. And I hope that "Worldwide Crush," the biggest-selling song by a teenage male solo artist since Justin Bieber's 2010 hit song "Baby" (source: *TeenTalk* online), stays at number one for the whole school year.

Thanks for listening,
Millie

After turning out my light, I quickly check his Flutter account. I wasn't allowed to use Flutter until last year. And truthfully, before Rory Calhoun, I had no reason to. I never post. And I don't really comment either; I'm not even sure what I'm supposed to say.

Tonight, it's like he's talking directly to me:

@rorycalhoun
Goodbye, summer! And good luck to everyone starting school tomorrow! #imissschool

It's almost like a kiss good night.

chapter 2

I wake up on the first day of school not with the gentle ring of an alarm clock but to the sound of AC/DC, that band from the eighties that is beloved by middle-aged white guys everywhere, including my dad. This is his first-day-of-school tradition.

He comes into my room in the same bathrobe he's had my entire life, his brown bed-head hair smushed up into horns on the side of his head, and launches into the air guitar routine he's been practicing since high school. And whenever they sing the words "back in black," my dad sings, "Back to *schooool!*" I look to make sure my curtains are closed.

Then he takes his routine to Billy's room, who thinks it's hilarious. I can hear him cracking up all the way down the hall. Today is Billy's first day of kindergarten, and we are all a little freaked out by how this tiny person, on the planet for such a short time, will now board a school bus by himself and go to school. My mom helped him pick out his clothes last night, and I heard her trying to convince him that the Darth Vader mask should not be included. I'll be curious to see what comes walking out of there.

At the kitchen table, we have a rare family breakfast, including Cheryl. Cheryl is my grandma, but she won't let me call her Grandma. I have to call her Cheryl. She says the word "grandma" is a self-fulfilling prophecy that makes women get tight perms and orthopedic shoes. She actually got orthopedic shoes last year for her back, but she calls them her foot levelers. Like maybe young people have foot levelers, but old people have orthopedic shoes.

Cheryl lives in Falling Waters Retirement Village, but she's staying with us while they renovate her condo.

She squeezes in next to me on a plastic chair that goes with the picnic table outside; our kitchen table is only meant for four, so we only have four real chairs. "Who's excited today?" she says, after doing her shot of Mountain Dew. Every morning she drinks a tiny cup of Mountain Dew. That, and she sleeps with a Target bag tied on her head like a turban. It's to prevent frizz, and she swears it works. I just wish she would take the Target bag off before coming to the breakfast table. "Billy," she says, "can you believe you are a real schoolboy? You're gonna love it; just ask your sister."

"It's true," I say. "Kindergarten is awesome."

"I *loved* kindergarten." Cheryl looks dreamy when she says this. "Ah, the smell of paste in the morning! When I was a girl, children used to eat paste. But I never did, of course." She carefully takes a sip of her coffee.

"Don't eat paste, Billy," my mom says, frantically buttering her toast. She knows how Billy hears things, so I'm sure she's worried he will now think eating paste is a good idea.

"I don't think they have paste anymore," I add. I haven't seen paste in years. We had a jar of paste at Florence Nightingale Elementary School, but no one ever used it. It was hard, like cement. Like maybe it had been there for several generations, but no one bothered to throw it away.

"What do you mean, they don't have paste?" Cheryl puts down her coffee cup. "How do you stick things together? Don't you stick things together anymore?"

"They have glue sticks," I say.

"Huh. I'll have to ask the Google about these 'glue sticks.'" This is how Cheryl looks things up on the Internet—she "asks the Google."

My mom eats her breakfast. In between bites, she takes pictures of Billy eating his breakfast on his first day of kindergarten. But I'm pretty sure he'll eat breakfast tomorrow and look exactly the same. No one takes pictures of me eating my breakfast.

"Millie, did you walk Pringles?" She snaps another picture of Billy drinking milk.

"No! Oh no!" How could I forget? I have been walking my beloved dog, Pringles, after toothbrushing and before breakfast for like thousands of days in a row . . . Now I'm realizing how nervous I might be for my first day of seventh grade. "Pringles!" I call out, and start shoving toast in my mouth as fast as I can.

"Don't worry, dear," Cheryl says. "I'll walk her today. You have a big day too." She pats my hand. She's always good at knowing stuff about me.

I swallow my toast and relax a little, trying to chew thoroughly so I don't get a stomachache. Last year, my advisory teacher told us that being nervous can give you a stomachache. Before she said that, I never got stomachaches; now I get them all the time. Thank you, advisory teacher. So I take relaxing breaths through my nose while I chew, trying not to blow crumbs out my mouth.

"Bus time!" my dad calls from the kitchen counter, where he is standing eating his toast. He is like the bus alarm. And we all jump up and run to the mudroom—my mom and dad and Billy and me. We scramble for shoes, kicking summer flip-flops out of the way and looking for shoes that have a mate close by. I don't know how shoes get separated when your feet are always side by side when you take them off. My mom finally settles on a pair of my dad's running shoes and starts pushing Billy toward the door. I grab my backpack and follow, yanking on my Rory Calhoun zipper pull as I go. My dad pulls his phone out of his pocket, aiming it at Billy and my mom, recording the moment.

Because Billy's bus comes just three minutes before my bus, I can easily walk him to his each morning and then wait for mine. But today, my mom and dad go with us as if they are marching Billy off to war or something. My dad alternately walks behind and then runs ahead, taking pictures of them, my mom holding Billy's hand, like she's putting him on the space shuttle instead of a school bus. I assume I'm in some of the pictures because I was in the general vicinity, but that would be purely coincidental.

When the bus comes, Billy reaches above his head and grabs the handrails with both hands, hoisting himself and his giant backpack onto the first step. Good thing he isn't wearing his Darth Vader mask, or he surely would've fallen over backward. We watch him walk down the aisle, just the top half of his head visible, holding our breath until a big kid finds him a seat. As the bus pulls away, he spies us out the window and gives us a little wave with his fingers . . . and we wave . . . and wave . . . and wave . . . until we can't see him anymore.

"Quick! Let's get the car!" My mom starts running.

"What? What are you talking about?" my dad shouts after her.

My mom turns around and says, "We can follow the bus! Come *on!*"

"Good idea!" And my dad starts running, too, without so much as a handshake for good luck.

"Umm . . . bye," I say to no one.

Not twenty seconds later, I see our family automobile

peel out and chase down the bus, whose job it is to safely transport school children to their destination. My dad's arm extends out of the passenger side window, holding his phone in the air . . . Oh God, he's taking video. I pray there are no cops on bus duty this morning, because this looks more like stalking than parenting.

At the height of my humiliation, Shauna arrives and says, "Is that your grandma?" She points to the lady waving to me from across the street—wearing fluffy slippers, a flowered robe, and a Target bag on her head—pulling on the leash of a reluctant, overweight bulldog.

This is not the best way to start a new school year.

"Go get 'em, sweetie!" she yells across the street, just in case people hadn't already noticed the lady with the plastic bag on her head. At least she acknowledges me, which is more than I can say for my parents.

I feel the rumble of the bus before I see it come around the corner. The door opens and we climb the steps absentmindedly, like obedient soldiers, because we've been doing it every day for seven years. Shauna follows me down the aisle on the way to our regular seat. Fourth row, right side—far away from the future criminals in the back but not so close to the driver that we look like babies.

Shauna watches everyone file by our seat and says, "Apparently it's National Rory Calhoun Appreciation Day, and I didn't get the memo. Did you get the memo?"

In everyone's arms, I see Rory Calhoun notebooks, Rory Calhoun folders, Rory Calhoun pencil cases—Shauna is right, his face is everywhere. Except for my zipper pull, there is no Rory Calhoun visible anywhere on my person. I explicitly requested plain notebooks and plain colored folders because I wasn't sure of what's cool and what's not this year. It changes all the time, and if you make a mistake (like wearing a unicorn T-shirt past the appropriate grade—speaking from personal experience), you could get noticed. In middle school, getting noticed is generally a bad thing. Last year, Drew Garza noticed that my Spanish textbook had the name Fred Washington stamped on the inside cover. So he called me Fred Washington the whole semester. And he told all the boys in gym that my name was Fred Washington; no matter what game we played, they were always shouting for someone to get Fred Washington out. Seriously, *why*?!

But my mom can't help herself, and she buys me one Rory Calhoun folder anyway—and I keep it tucked away in my dresser drawer for very special items I want to save. It's nice, actually, to have this secret picture of him to look at each time I want to save something special.

Shauna scrunches down in the seat and puts her knees against the seat in front of us, so I do the same. Her overalls cover up what I know is her Madame President T-shirt, and she pulls one of her glossy pigtails out of her backpack strap. If I wore pigtails, I'm sure I would look like a kindergartner, but when she does it, it looks cool.

She leans over and whispers in my ear, "Did you see that Amina Gale and Sam Herkim are sitting together?"

I casually turn around and see them sitting silently next to each other, scrolling on their phones.

"Is it on purpose or by accident?" I whisper back.

"It's on purpose. They started dating yesterday."

I look at them again. "Didn't he throw a dodgeball at her head in third grade?"

Shauna shrugs and rolls her eyes, which means yes, he did.

And now she's dating him? Clearly, I don't get dating.

chapter 3

I find my locker, 238M, and pull out my plain notebooks and my plain folders and put them on the shelf. Glancing behind me at the people walking the hallways, I very nonchalantly tape one Rory Calhoun face to the back wall where only I can see it. It's small. But I know it's there. Across the hall, Trinity Breen is trying to fit a full-size poster inside her locker, crunching a big crease across Rory's forehead.

I take a deep breath and step out into the crowd, making my way to my first class. Middle school hallways can be intimidating; at what point in elementary school do you have every single student in the hallway at the same time, racing to be somewhere in the next four minutes? Almost never. And when, in elementary school, do you see people—and by people, I mean children—who look like full-grown adults, with peach-fuzz mustaches or boobs. And they might be exactly the same age as someone with no peach-fuzz mustache or no boobs. I swear, there are some boys in my class who still need help cutting their meat and some who look like they're ready to join the army or something. It's like a petri dish of puberty. "Puberty" is such a gross word. I hate it, especially when people say "poo-berty." I wish everyone would stop talking about poo-berty, but they can't because it's walking around everywhere in the hallways at my school.

First hour, advisory. Second hour, language arts. By third hour, Earth science, I'm starving and get distracted by the boy across from me eating gummy worms behind his book. He smiles at me, and I look down quickly, pretending to take notes, writing the words to "Worldwide Crush" as quickly as I can because I don't actually know what the teacher just said.

After Earth science, I wait in the lunchroom for Shauna. The lunchroom is in the basement, so it has no windows; it kind of feels like a food prison. They've painted it really bright colors—orange and yellow and turquoise—but it still feels like a food prison. Last year, we always sat in the back by the food pyramid posters, underneath the hanging mobile of healthy snacks. According to the mobile, we should be snacking on apples, bananas, and something that looks like a chaff of wheat.

I practice my signature while I wait; I'm trying out a new M that I think looks very scripty and Gothic, like someone from a British PBS series. I write, "Millie Jackson, Millie Jackson, Millie Jackson." And then, feeling very daring, I write . . . "Millie Calhoun."

I stare at that name like it's a work of art.

Millie Calhoun.

I want to say it out loud, but I'm too smart for that, so I just mouth the words, moving my mouth but hearing it only in my head. It sounds better too! "Millie Jackson" sounds like you're plodding down a sidewalk, but "Millie Calhoun" sounds like you're jumping on a trampoline.

Mrs. Millie Calhoun. Oh, sigh.

"Nobody changes their name anymore, especially if you want to be famous."

"Gob! Shauna, you scared me! Don't sneak up on me like that!" I'm very proud to say that last year I started saying

"Gob" as an expletive, and it totally worked. It worked so well that other people started using it too. And then it spread, and now everybody uses it. Okay, not everybody, but a lot of people. More than just me anyway. Gob!

"It's true," Shauna says, setting her lunch tray down. "Famous women never change their names. Why can't men change *their* names? Besides, when my parents decided to name me Shauna, they tried it on with Mendez, not the name of some random guy they won't meet for thirty years. Although I've probably seen my dad like three times since I was little, so maybe he shouldn't have gotten a vote in the first place."

"I was just playing around," I say, crossing out the Millie Calhoun. "And I like the name Shauna for you."

"I do too, actually. I'm just cranky today. How are you supposed to grow up Filipino when the Filipino part of your parentage ditches you? No offense, Angie."

Angie is Shauna's mom. She's mostly Norwegian, I think.

"I'm sorry," I say. "I keep thinking he'll invite you to the Philippines for Christmas or something."

"Don't hold your breath. 'Lower your expectations, Shauna.' That's what my mom says. And also," she looks back at my notebook, "nobody uses 'Mrs.' anymore. Just scratch that. It's nobody's business if you're married or not."

"And now I have no idea what you're talking about." She's jumping around, and I can't keep up. That's not uncommon, actually. Her brain just moves faster than mine.

"Men don't have to tell people if they're married, so why should we? We just call them 'Mr.' no matter what. All professional women use 'Ms.' these days."

"What about Mrs. McCauley? And Mrs. Neaton? And Mrs. Swartz?" I had to go to speech therapy in second grade when I was in Mrs. Swartz's class. I had a lisp, and it was really hard to hide a lisp in Mrs. Swartz's class because of the difficulty in saying "Mrs. Swartz."

"I think teachers are exempt," Shauna says. "But when you go to a board meeting at the bank, no one introduces the boss as 'Mrs. Banker.'"

"Well . . . what am I supposed to write on my notebook then?"

"Just stick with the standard 'Millie + Rory.' It's classic. You could add 'forever,' but that's not super realistic. What is this stuff?" She picks up a piece of meat on her tray and examines it. "It said 'turkey roll-up and vegetable medley' on the menu, but this does not resemble turkey, and it's not rolled up."

A round white boy with peach fuzz on his upper lip walks toward us, holding a tray in front of his body, and stops right in front of Shauna.

"Good afternoon, lovely ladies of Susan B. Anthony! What is it we're discussing at this prodigious lunch hour?" Our friend Carson uses words I have to look up in the dictionary. "Prodigious" means remarkably or impressively great in extent, size, or degree. He puts his tray down across from Shauna and eyes my notebook with the crossed-out Millie Calhoun on it.

I quickly slide it into my backpack. "Weather," I say. "Discussing weather. And politics. But mostly weather. There are no tornadoes in the forecast today, are there, Shauna?"

"No, Millie, there are no tornadoes in the forecast today." She looks at me like, *Get over yourself, weirdo.*

Carson and I went to preschool together a million years ago at Neighborhood Friends Nursery School. We were in Teacher Tina's class, also known as The Yellow Room.

Carson looks up from his tray just as a small boy (no peach fuzz) appears by our table, hoping for a spot. "Ladies and gentlemen," Carson announces, "please make room for the lunch tray of the venerable Hawthorne B. Awesome!"

"Venerable" means accorded a great deal of respect, especially because of age, wisdom, or character.

I slide down and let Hawthorne sit next to me. Hawthorne and Carson come as a team. If you see Carson, Hawthorne is likely lurking in his shadow.

"Hi, Hawthorne," I say.

"Hi, Millie. Did you have a good summer?" His nose sounds just a little bit stuffy.

"Yeah. I suppose. If you count riding my bike to the library every day to check out biographies of former child stars who died of drug overdoses as a good summer. Then yes, it was awesome. Does anyone want my applesauce packet?"

"Yes, please! Thank you, milady!" Carson reaches out for my applesauce and puts it in the rectangular divot next to his milk.

I used to play with Carson and Hawthorne in the summertime. Now that we've grown up, it's different, though. Sometimes they just hang out on their bikes in front of my house. And last year, they helped me get past this crazy cat that thought she owned my driveway. It was really sweet how they caused a ruckus and distracted the cat so I could run to my door. But I'm not sure about being friends with boys in seventh grade—even if it's just at the lunch table or on the bus. There's just so much Fred Washington one girl can take.

But I am also aware that, if it weren't for Shauna, I would be alone in this lunchroom, and I live in fear of someone switching our schedules. Sitting by yourself in the lunchroom is probably one of the worst things I can think of. It's just you, awkwardly putting food in your mouth, while everyone watches and wonders why you have no friends.

I saw you standing all alone,
Holding your worries in your hands,
Without a soft place to land.
And I knew you needed a friend.

We are *all* by ourselves,
Though it doesn't look that way to you.
You're not the only one,
I promise you.
You're not the only one.

So I won't let you wander
All alone in the crowd,
I won't let you feel unwanted.

I hope my smile says it all.
There's a place for you right here.
And you can . . .
Come sit by me.

—from "Come Sit by Me"
Music and lyrics by Rory Calhoun

chapter 4

On the bus ride home, Shauna and I do "the takeaway," as my dad says. In other words, we talk through our first day and summarize our findings. Carson and Hawthorne have the seat in front of us, and they're doing the same thing. Carson has a textbook open on his lap, and he's complaining about polyglot, this weird class where you study a bunch of languages at once.

"Polyglot has already eluded me," he says. "This map has nary a trace of Japan on it. Where art thou, Japan? Where art thou?!"

"Ask Shauna," Hawthorne says, pointing behind him.

"Dude—I'm not from Japan. How the bleep should I know?"

"Oh. Yeah . . . I just thought . . . because you're . . . um, forget it." His voice trails off, and he turns to look out the window. I think I see his ears getting pink.

Shauna looks at me and we roll our eyes. Stuff like this happens to Shauna all the time. She's the only Filipino kid in our school, and she always gets lumped together with the Korean kids and the Vietnamese kids and that one Chinese kid. And apparently Japanese kids too, even though we don't have any.

We hit a speed bump and bounce up in our seats just as Carson yells, "Huzzah!"

I think that means he found Japan.

As the bus turns into Walnut Grove Estates, I talk faster so I can finish my takeaway before it lets me off on Laura Lane. Our neighborhood is named after *Little House on the Prairie*, which means "pioneer girl" is a very popular Halloween costume around here. It's also perfect for Cheryl, who says Pa Ingalls is sexy—not the book Pa, the TV one. If you don't know who that is, go ask the Google; you'll find a pioneer man who likes to take his shirt off a lot. So anyway, here's my takeaway on day one of seventh grade:

First hour is advisory with Ms. Peterman. She is young and wears cool T-shirts and always smiles and says, "Hey, *you!*" when she sees you. I like that. Advisory is only twenty minutes, and we don't really learn or anything—we just take attendance and "orient ourselves to our learning environment." But still, she seems like someone who could help me if I had an embarrassing question or something.

She gets an A-plus for being sweet and pretty and happy to see us.

Second hour, I have language arts with Ms. Hempel, but she wants us to call her Mary. My mom says she is a hippie, which I guess is kind of cool, like she's a rebel from the sixties or something. She is a little bit old, like a young grandma, and she has long, straight hair that she sometimes wears in a side braid or on top of her head in a knot, always with a real flower tucked behind her ear. A real flower! Every day! And all of her jewelry makes noise—her dangly earrings or her shiny bangles or, I swear to God, her ankle bracelets. She is like a jingle factory. She smells a little funny but nice funny, like a hair salon mixed with a bonfire. She is *super* excited about all of the *wonderful* pieces of *literature* that we will get to *explore*! *Together!*

I give her an A-minus for originality and enthusiasm. Points deducted for possible distraction by her jewelry jingles and because she seems like she might want us to talk about our feelings, and that could get uncomfortable.

Third hour is Earth science with Mr. Rajput—snore. Science is not my favorite, and Earth science seems like it might be very brown; earth is brown, brown is a boring color, therefore Earth science will not be exciting or interesting in any way. Mr. Rajput is a little uptight and doesn't seem like he's that into Earth science. It's more like he's into giving tests or grading things.

I give Mr. Rajput a C for boring subject matter and seeming like he doesn't like us very much.

Then comes lunch with Shauna (thank God!) and outdoor free-choice time. Apparently, we are too old to have recess but not too old for outdoor free-choice time. Explain that one to me, please.

Fourth hour I have math. Gob! For the first time, I am *not* in the highest math group. I am in the second-to-the-highest math group, which makes me feel a little bit bad. I don't know what happened. All I know is that my teacher is not Ms. Croutemeier, who is known as the teacher of smart math kids, and that all the kids in my old math class aren't with me anymore—they all have Ms. Croutemeier. I have Mr. Sneed, and I'm with kids like Aveda and Almay, the twins who smell so good. They are pretty smart but not *really* smart, and I would be lying if I said that didn't hurt my feelings a little bit, or maybe a lot.

I give Mr. Sneed a D for not being Ms. Croutemeier.

Fifth hour is specialist time, and I rotate between information media (that's library time), movement studies (that's gym), artistic mindscapes (that's art), polyglot (that language thing), and general music (that's music, duh).

And sixth hour, the last hour of the day, is social studies with Dr. Marion. Why a doctor is teaching social studies, I have no idea. I've been told she's not really a *doctor* doctor but a doctor of education. An education doctor? I don't get it. But that is what she tells people to call her, so what am I supposed to do? More importantly, she is super nice, and she laughs really loudly, and she promised we would get to do "lots of exciting projects that will allow us to explore our interests."

I give Dr. Marion a B-plus for making me look forward to social studies, even though it doesn't seem all that interesting.

When I get off the bus, I see smoke coming out of the window of my old playhouse in the backyard. I'm not worried; I know it's Cheryl in there smoking. Cheryl is a closet smoker. She thinks it's a well-kept secret, but everyone knows and pretends they don't. She officially let me in on her secret when I was in fifth grade, and I thought my playhouse was burning down. I ran out there and stuck the garden hose in the window, full blast, before realizing it was a grandma, not a fire. I found her sitting on a plastic stool, leaning against my play stove with a cigarette in her hand, dripping hose water from her hair.

"Don't ever smoke, dear," was all she said.

"I know," I replied. "I wasn't planning on it."

"Don't look at me like that," she said. "I'm a grandma, I can do what I want." Then she took a long drag and blew it toward the ceiling, water dripping onto her shoulders. I guess the hose missed the cigarette.

Today when I see the smoke, I know it's just Cheryl on a smoke break, and I let myself into the house. I drop my backpack on the floor in the mudroom and grab my phone out of the front pocket, stepping over shoes, a bucket of sand toys, and one hockey skate that sat there all summer. It dings in my hand, and I see a notification from Rory's Flutter account. During the summer, I checked Rory's posts and messages constantly. At school, it's so much harder to keep up. He could've written his whole life story in that amount of time.

@rorycalhoun
Check out the special Back to School feature on *TeenTalk* online! Might be a little personal? #blushing

Oh my God, what teenage boy blushes?! He's so flipping adorable. I tap the link.

....

TeenTalk Exclusive!

Are you the girl for Rory Calhoun?
He gives us the real scoop in his latest interview!

TT: Word on the street is that you're single and looking. True or false?

RC: I am definitely single. And I, like everyone else, would really like a girlfriend. Oh man, that's embarrassing! I think my face is red right now.

TT: Do you have any turn-ons?

RC: Hats. As long as you're not trying to be something you're not, hats can be really sexy.

TT: Turnoffs?

RC: Someone who won't leave the house without full hair and makeup. Just do what I do—put a hat on (see "turn-ons" listed above).

TT: Favorite first date?

RC: If I'm at home, I love walking on the beach. Most of the time, I'm by myself—but I'd love to share that with someone.

TT: Second date?

RC: Playing Yahtzee at my house.

TT: Third date?

RC: That's private!

I run upstairs and pull out my RC diary.

Dear RC,

After a game of Yahtzee, we could walk down to the beach. I stuff my frizzy ponytail into my hat and jog along beside you in the sand, wiping sweat from my makeup-less face. I smile at you out of the corner of my eye, but I am nonchalant, completely without anxiety of any kind, and I stop to kick in the surf, spraying you with water. "Hey!" you say, laughing and playfully putting your arms around me. From behind your back, you pull out a flower, holding it shyly in front of me.

"I would really like a girlfriend," you say.

Could this be me?

Love and stuff,
Millie

P.S. Found a hat I want online. It's a coonskin cap with a tail hanging off the back. It looks outdoorsy, like something you'd wear for a walk on the beach. I will order and try it at home for a while to see how it goes.

chapter 5

"Dinnertime!" I can hear my mom all the way down in the kitchen.

"What are we having?!" I call back from my room. I'm in the middle of writing an acrostic poem with the letters R-O-R-Y-C-A-L-H-O-U-N, and I don't want to interrupt my flow. For each of the letters in his name, I have to come up with a word that describes him. As lovable as he is, that still takes some concentration.

"For you? Worms!" For some reason, my mom gets all huffy when I ask her what we're having for dinner. But I can't stop asking.

Reluctantly, I get up off my bed, put my notebook and my pens on my desk, and move toward my door, touching my hand to Rory's paper chest as I pass my closet—a hand-to-poster hug. I make my way toward the kitchen and poke my head around the corner—just my head, not my body—a power move to show I'm cooperating but not all the way.

She sees my face and gives me an annoyed look. "If you must know so urgently, we are having bacon and eggs," she says.

I try hard not to comment, because I really don't want bacon and eggs. Some people think having breakfast for dinner is just so fun, but I have to disagree. I just want dinner for dinner.

Cheryl comes in with Billy and helps him into the booster seat that allows him to reach the table. His Darth Vader mask wobbles on his neck as he gets settled. When Cheryl picked him up at the bus today after his first day of kindergarten, he raced in the door and went straight for the mask. When you're a regular Darth Vader–mask wearer, I guess six hours is a long time to go without wearing your Darth Vader mask.

"Billy, can you take off the mask for dinner, please?" my mom asks.

"Oh, Carrie, sweetheart, he hasn't worn it all day. I don't mind having Darth Vader at the dinner table with me." Cheryl gives Darth Vader a kiss on his plastic cheek.

"Cheryl, Darth Vader doesn't have a mouth. How will he get the food in his mouth?"

"What if I take my cape off instead?" Billy says, trying to negotiate.

"Honey," my mom says to him. "How does that help you get the food in your mouth?"

"Fine," Cheryl says. "Billy, give me your Darth Vader mask, and I'll put it in a safe place for you. You keep the cape, though, little guy."

My dad walks in from the garage just as we are sitting down. He pulls out his chair and says to Billy, "Hey, buddy— where's your Darth Vader mask?"

My mom looks at him like, *Are you kidding me?* and says, "Please, can we just eat?" Then she puts bacon on my plate, even though I didn't ask for it. That's when Billy holds up his plate and says casually, "May I please have some goddamn bacon?"

We all freeze. My mom looks at my dad. My dad looks at my mom. And Cheryl looks at them both like she just saw Elvis in the backyard. And do you know what my mom does? She puts some goddamn bacon on his plate. Totally serious—like her tiny kindergartner didn't just swear at the dinner table in his booster seat.

Cheryl takes in a sharp breath and says, "It must be kindergarten! Where on earth would he hear language like that?"

My mom whispers out of the side of her mouth, "Don't make a big deal of it, Cheryl. If we ignore it, it will go away." Then she nonchalantly takes another bite of her goddamn bacon. My dad does the same.

"Children shouldn't swear," Cheryl whispers. "Show me a kid who swears, and I'll show you a kid who doesn't wash his hands after he poops. They're disease mongers."

"Oh please," my mom says, out loud this time. "You scolding people for swearing is like a fish scolding people for swimming."

This is true. Cheryl swears like a sailor.

"I said *children* who swear. That's totally different. I'm a grandma, I can say what I want, goddamn it . . ."

Billy holds his bacon up to the sky and says, in his best Darth Vader voice, "Goddamn it!"

My dad looks at her and says "Really, Cheryl? You still think it's kindergarten?"

"Well, I'm tired," she says. "I save my precious energy for things like breathing and circulation. If I start holding it in, you could come home and find me dead of an aneurysm."

Cheryl is very knowledgeable about curse words, and she actually helps me come up with good replacements. "Anybody can say shit," she says. "But it takes a clever person to yell, 'Sheboygan, Wisconsin!' Even a simple 'Schmidt!' will keep you out of trouble. Or what about 'Frank'? You could save that for when you need to use the big one."

My mom tries to change the subject. "Somebody, please—tell Dad about the first day of school."

I take a breath to speak, but their eyes are all on Billy.

He says, "There's a girl with a blue shirt."

"That's great, honey!" My mom is all over this news. "What's her name?"

"I don't know."

"Tomorrow you should ask her what her name is."

"Yeah," he says, clearly not listening. He's more interested in dipping his goddamn bacon in egg yolk at this point.

But my mom and dad keep asking him questions anyway: "Is your teacher nice?" "What did you play?" "Did you go to the bathroom while you were there?" "Were you able to snap your pants by yourself?"

No one asks me any questions. I take the opportunity to glance down at my phone, hidden under my napkin. A text buzzes silently on my lap.

Shauna: Go to TTO. NOW!
Me: TTO?
Shauna: *TeenTalk* online, floofus!
Me: Why? What? Tell me! You're a floofus!
Shauna: No, you're a floofus, and we could seriously marry Rory Calhoun. For real. Check it out, and text me back.

....

TeenTalk Online Exclusive!

Rory Calhoun Confesses:
You Might Be His Worldwide Crush!

TT: "Worldwide Crush" is said to be the biggest song by a teen solo artist since fourteen-year-old Justin Bieber. Be honest, Rory—is this song about you?

RC: Yeah, it's hard. When you travel the world with a bunch of adults, performing in a different city every single night, you don't get many opportunities to get to know people your own age. I love what I do. I love making music and singing to my fans, seriously love it—but I'm really missing something that every guy wants, you know? That one special person who makes everything okay, who's there for me when I'm sad or worried . . . that person you just want to be close to all the time.

All the people my age are in the audience, and I just feel like somebody out there is the one for me.

But how am I ever going to find her?

My hand grips my phone. I hold it like I'm holding the very words I just read. I have loved Rory Calhoun forever. *Forever.* And now, with these words before me, Rory Calhoun is telling me that I'm not childish and stupid for wanting to be with him. He's looking for the same thing I am. And he's looking in a place that I plan to be.

"Millie?"

My mom's voice startles me, and I quickly grab some bacon to put in my mouth, like I've been eating bacon this whole time.

"Are you on your phone at the dinner table?" she asks.

I shake my head and continue to put bacon in my mouth. Shaking my head is less of a lie than saying no out loud. Plus, my phone was never at the table; it was under the table.

"Are you on your phone *under* the table?" she says.

Gob. I don't shake my head again because doing that twice would equal saying no out loud. And that would be lying.

"Maybe her napkin is just super compelling, Carrie," my dad offers. "It could be that she's staring at her lap because her napkin is just that interesting."

"So tell us, Millie, what is it in your lap that is so interesting that it makes you completely disregard the 'no phones at the dinner table' rule? I don't have my phone. Dad doesn't have his phone."

"I have my phone," says Cheryl. "But no one ever calls me."

What am I supposed to say? That I just might marry the guy on my bedroom poster? This is life changing for me, but it would sound ridiculous to her.

I look at my mom and fib, "Shauna is providing me with some book recommendations."

"Is that right?" she says, skeptically.

"Yep."

"About what?"

"About . . . strong women in American history."

"Is that so?"

"And climate change . . ."

"Oh, I'm sure. Yeah, I'm going to need your phone tonight," she says. "You can get it back tomorrow."

Frank!

Chapter 6

At exactly 12:01 a.m., I sneak downstairs to where my phone is plugged in. Because technically, it's tomorrow, when my mom said I could have my phone back. Plus, I'm not unplugging it—I'm just standing at the kitchen counter looking at it while it's plugged in. That hardly counts as using my phone.

Someone has posted a video from tonight's concert in Copenhagen, Denmark.

I tap the triangle and wait for it to load.

Loading . . .

Loading . . .

My heart pounds in my chest like I'm waiting for him in the real audience.

The video begins, and people are screaming. I can actually feel the screaming vibrating in my hand. And there's this light that flashes to the beat of a drum, so bright, like the sun is turning on and off right over the front of the stage. There's a row of dancers, the Rory Pack, holding a pose but pulsing along with the drumbeat, like they're waiting too—the waiting is killing me! The screaming gets louder and louder.

And then, all at once, a boom, a flash, an explosion of confetti, and Rory Calhoun appears—how?! I have no idea!—at the front of the stage, leading the dancers as the music for "Love Me" begins. Gob! I love this song! People lose their minds, and he's not even singing yet! It's hard to be still because I totally know this choreography from watching the music video.

He's dressed very simply, just a white T-shirt and a pair of jeans that hug him so nicely. The jeans have these weird sparkles in them, just a few here and there, and they twinkle when the light hits them just right.

When it's time to sing, he moves to the very front of the stage, and he looks up and opens his arms wide like he's serenading everyone in the cheap seats. And the crowd *roars*. It sounds like thunder. It surprises Rory, and he stops and laughs during the musical bridge and puts his hand on his heart like, *I can't believe this!*

I replay it a couple of times, just that last part, so I can see his surprised and happy face. And I feel that warming in my chest that makes me know I love him. I close my eyes so I can sit in this feeling for a minute.

When I open them, I see there's a video for just about every song in the concert. I could be up all night watching this stuff. But I have a quiz in second hour tomorrow, and Ms. Hempel—I mean, Mary—just gave us a talking-to about how sleep is the most important element in your study routine. I decide to watch just two more: "Come Sit by Me" and "Sunshine Girl."

And then . . . oh, wait . . . at the bottom, I see "Worldwide Crush." The song that now gives me and millions of others hope.

I open it.

The music begins, and Rory reaches his hand out to a girl in the audience—in the front row, just to his left. She takes his hand, and he leads her up the steps, onto the stage, and next to him—oh good Lord, I can hardly stand it—where there's a stool waiting for her, and she sits down. I'm not dancing anymore. I'm perfectly still, paralyzed by the notion that some real-life girl is living my fantasy. He starts to sing, right at her face, looking in her eyes . . .

"I travel the world to find you, I'm searching for your face in the crowd. Is it you who's gonna make me feel alright? Is it you? Is it you?"

And she starts to cry.

"Won't you look into my eyes? Please find me, please find me. Won't you help me realize that you'll find me, you'll find me? I can feel it in my heart that you're out there. You're my crush, my crush, my crush . . . my worldwide crush."

The girl is full-on sobbing now. And he wraps his arms around her to comfort her and places a soft kiss on her cheek.

The cell phone pans around to show that all the girls in the seats are also crying.

And so am I.

I could be that girl.

Oh please, let me be that girl.

Dear RC,

Real, so real—not fake, or flashy.
Omigod, I love your smile because you have . . .
Really white teeth.
Your face is so sad when you talk about Sgt. Pepper,
your beloved dog who died.
Casual and carefree, not saggy, are your clothes.
Abs, just a peek, when you raise your arms high in the
video for "Sunshine Girl."
Lashes, thick and dark, like a warm blanket of love.
Hair the color of morning cereal: Super Golden Sugar
Smacks.
On my closet door, wishing me a good night's sleep.
Unbelievably kind, in a way that boys aren't.
Never not love you.

Love and stuff,
Millie

Before going back to bed, I read the interview in *Teen-Talk* one more time. I close my eyes and try to think of some words to say that would be like a prayer . . . or a wish . . . like a wishing prayer thing. I assume it's more effective if I address it to someone specific like God or Jesus or something like that. And I wonder about folding my hands—is that required? I decide yes. So I fold my hands and say silently to myself, *Dear God (or Jesus or whatever), please let me be in the audience someday. And let him see me.*

I don't want God to laugh at me, so I avoid saying things like "marry" or "girlfriend" or "live-in lover." Also, I'm assuming that a prayer-y thing is more likely to be answered if I don't ask for too much. I'm just guessing here, because I have exactly no experience with churchy things. Would it have killed my parents to take me to Sunday school just once? But it also occurs to me that, if I'm thinking it in my head, God knows anyway. So I end quickly with, *Okay. Bye. And thank you.*

Today could change everything. I am just a regular seventh grader living on Laura Lane in Walnut Grove Estates, but even a girl from a boring suburb in Minnesota who has never traveled beyond Wisconsin—unless you count Arizona, which I don't because it's just my great-grandma's condo, and there's nothing to do there except float in the pool with old ladies (no splashing allowed)—has as good a chance as anyone to be the one he's looking for. All I have to do is go to a concert. If he really and truly feels that there's true love waiting for him in the audience, I just don't know why it couldn't be me.

Dear RC,

Just prayed to God/Jesus. This is serious.

Love for real,
Millie

chapter 7

GOOD MORNING USA
KRTV NEWS
AUGUST 26
7:01 A.M.

Faith Franklin, a.m. anchor: Good morning, USA. I'm Faith Franklin, and here are today's headlines. Rory Calhoun, the teenage pop star known for his good looks and his enthusiastic fans, thrilled young people around the world yesterday when he revealed in an interview that his song "Worldwide Crush" was actually about his own real-life wish to find love in the audience. Following the release of the interview, which was published online at TeenTalk Weekly, remaining tickets for his European and Japanese shows sold out within hours. Dates for Calhoun's US tour have not yet been announced, and US fans took to social media, pushing the hashtag #rorycomehere into the top five trending hashtags of all time. "Worldwide Crush" continues to hold the number one spot after five weeks on the Billboard music chart. In political news today . . .

"We're going, right?" I say to Shauna on the bus. "We have to do this together. I'll need you to hold my hand or scream with me or . . . I don't know, just swear to me we won't miss this."

I'm already picturing us getting ready for the concert in my room—doing each other's hair, maybe something cool we saw online like a fancy braidy thing. I picture us wearing bras. Well, I picture us *needing* bras. I try not to look down at my chest, which I know, even without looking, is not super hilly. There are some slight inclines here and there but nothing that requires a real bra with hooks and things. Which is fine! I just don't want to look like a third grader.

"Well," Shauna says, "yes. But that's assuming he actually comes here for a concert."

"Shauna! Don't even say that!"

"Millie . . . what if? What if he doesn't come here?"

Instead of responding, I pull out my phone, and for the first time ever, I comment on a Flutter post:

#rorycomehere
Please. Love, all your fans from Minnesota. And all the fans in neighboring states who come to Minnesota for concerts. And that's a lot of people!

Every time I go to my locker, I try to check Flutter for updates. But most of the time, it won't load. It just spins and spins—stupid phone. After school, I tap and scroll for hours, watching as people cheer for a concert in their hometown.

At dinner, with my phone hidden under the table, I see a headline that reads "Mayor of Chicago Posts on Social

Media #rorycomehere, Offers Unique Key to the City and Proclaims Rory Calhoun Day." I click on it and skim the article while Billy tells my parents about his bathroom habits at kindergarten.

> The mayor of Chicago has reached out to Rory Calhoun via Flutter, hoping to lure the young pop star to Chicago with an unusual and hyperlocal offering. He wrote, "Chicago awaits you with a giant key to the city, made from Chicago's own Gino's East pizza! Plus, I will proclaim concert day to be Rory Calhoun Day across the entire city of Chicago. #rorycomehere!"

I get caught again with my phone at/under the dinner table. But this time, I take a breath and tell the truth. "The mayor of Chicago offered Rory Calhoun the key to the city made out of pizza."

My mom holds out her hand, and I put my phone in the center of her palm.

After loading the dishwasher, I use an actual pencil and piece of paper, since I have no phone, to write out what I plan to send to the mayors of both St. Paul and Minneapolis, the two biggest cities near me:

> @minneapolismayor @stpaulmayor
> Chicago mayor offered Rory Calhoun key to the city made of pizza. What can we offer to get this life-changing concert opportunity? Please make it fun. Not like a fruit or veg. #rorycomehere

I will post it tonight at 12:01 a.m., when it is technically tomorrow. It will be my second social media comment ever.

But when I creep down the stairs in the dark, Cheryl is standing at the counter, sipping from a mug.

"Hello, sweetheart," she says. "Are you here for your phone?"

"No! I'm just . . ." I see her mug. "I came down for some tea."

"You don't drink tea. But I'll make you some anyway." She reaches over and presses the button on the electric kettle and grabs a mug from the drying rack on the counter.

Having Cheryl here has been surprisingly nice. She's like my mom but not; she's definitely in charge of me, but she talks to me instead of getting mad at me. In fact, I can't remember a single time in my whole life she's ever gotten mad at me. And if her condo renovation goes on for a long time, I'd be okay with that.

She's wearing her power walking tracksuit, the one she wears on walks with her Falling Waters Retirement Village friends. They used to power walk to the Burger King for milk-shakes, but now Cheryl's not allowed in the Burger King; there was an altercation involving some ladies from a rival retirement village. And now she's banned from the Burger King.

So now they power walk to the Burger King, and Cheryl waits in the parking lot while her friends go in and get her a milkshake. One time she walked up to the drive-through and tried to order a milkshake there, but it didn't work. "They said I wasn't allowed *in* the Burger King," she said. "I wasn't *in*. I was only *at*. Jackasses."

Now she plays with the zipper on her tracksuit while she drops a tea bag in my empty mug.

"Tell me, sweetheart, why are you having such trouble staying off your phone?"

"I don't know what the big deal is," I say. "No one else I know gets their phone taken away at the dinner table."

"Maybe no one else you know has a mom who enjoys her daughter's company so much."

"What? That's not it. She just doesn't understand . . ."

"No mother ever does, sweetheart, trust me."

"Exactly! She doesn't know how paralyzed I am without my phone! I feel like a pioneer girl, making butter for fun and missing out on all the barn dances in town. There's so much I need to do right now, and I'm completely powerless without my phone!"

She nods her head and hands me my mug of tea.

"Tell me what's so urgent right now."

"It's Rory Calhoun."

"Who's Rory Calhoun?"

"It's the guy in my magazine," I say. Even though Rory is probably the most famous teenager in the world right now, it's understandable that a grandma who mostly watches the news and reruns of *Little House on the Prairie* may not remember his name. So I get my *TeenTalk Weekly* magazine with the free poster inside, to remind her.

She grabs the magazine and looks at the cover. Immediately, she knows who it is and jabs her finger at his face. It bothers me just a little bit, the way she does that, like it could hurt him or something. "Oh yes!" she says. "The boy on your wall!"

"Yes, the boy on my wall." I smile and try to take the magazine, but she pulls it away so she can examine it more carefully.

"Oh Lordy . . . I've never looked at him this closely before . . . Except for the fact that he needs to run a brush through his hair, this boy is gorgeous! He's perfect! It's like they made him in a test tube! Oh, his freckles, you can barely see them! They're adorable!" She pulls the magazine to her chest and exclaims, "I wanna love him too!"

"Stop it," I say. "You're making fun of me now." I'm embarrassed, but I'm smiling.

"Well, he really is amazingly attractive. If I were about fifty years younger, I could date his dad. So what does this hunk do? . . . Is he a singer, a dancer, a magician? Tell me what's stolen your heart, dear."

"He's a singer." She's let go of the magazine now, so I casually slide it to my side of the table so she doesn't spill tea on it.

"Is that what you're listening to when you've got those things in your ears? I would probably know that if you kids didn't pipe the music directly into your brains through wires."

"Right now, I mostly listen to the same song over and over again because he talked about it in an interview. It's called 'Worldwide Crush,' and it's been the number one song for, like, weeks and weeks, but it's getting even more popular because he told this interviewer that the song was about him . . . about how being a performer on the road can be really hard because you can't meet people your age. And he sees so many people in the audience at his concerts every night that he finally realizes, 'Hey, I bet my future girlfriend could be out there, right in front of me.' You know, at one of his concerts."

Cheryl's eyes light up. "Well! My goodness! You have to go! How do we get you to one of these concerts?"

"Well, right now he's just doing concerts in Europe and Japan. And he hasn't announced all the cities for his US tour yet, so we don't know if he's coming here. It's driving everyone crazy. Cities are giving him pizza and chocolate and whoopie pies because they want him to come to their city so badly."

"What the schnitzel is a whoopie pie?" Cheryl says.

"It doesn't matter. The important part is that all of these cities are doing something to make him come in concert, and we haven't done anything. If I can get my phone, I can do something."

"That's pooey. What do you think we did before we carried telephones in our purses? Do you think we did nothing? You kids are so funny; I swear, someday they'll make a machine to brush your teeth, and no one will know how to brush their teeth anymore."

"So what should I do?"

"Write him a letter."

"Like an email?"

"No. Like a letter."

"What do you mean? Like on a piece of paper?"

Cheryl laughs while she takes a sip of tea. "Yes, honey, on a piece of paper. Write him a fan letter. Make it personal. Put it in the snail mail."

"But why? No one sends letters anymore."

"Exactly. That's why you do it. He probably gets millions of emails. He can't read all those! It's much harder to ignore something that you don't see very often. We used to do it all the time—the Beatles, the Monkees, all the big hunks."

"*You* had a crush?!"

"Oh my stars, yes. Paul McCartney will always turn my head. Even if he only lives in photographs. In fact, in 1964, I actually drove five hours to Milwaukee with my friend Carol to watch them drive by in a limo. Can you believe that?"

"Seriously? Your mom let you do that?"

"No! Grandma Phyllis had no idea," she says, waving her hand. "Grandma Phyllis thought I was at a slumber party with Carol. If she had known that Carol's parents were out of town and her older sister Barb had a new car and lots of time on her hands, she might've thought twice about that slumber party." She points her mug at me and says, "Honey, if I can sneak a trip to Milwaukee, the least you can do is write a letter."

"I do have really nice handwriting."

"Yes, you do! And you might be the only tweenager on the planet who does! Use your gifts!"

I blow on my tea and think about this. I bet Shauna would help me. She won the Susan B. Anthony Halloween story contest last year.

"This is really important stuff, Millie." Cheryl puts her mug down and pages through my *TeenTalk*. "Suppressing our feelings of love is very unhealthy. It's best to get it out there. Feel it and enjoy it! Not to mention that this is your first love affair; that's a huge milestone in a woman's life. It's a little one-sided right now, but that's not a bad thing at your age—he's like your poster boyfriend. And what an adorable poster boyfriend he is, am I right?" She looks down at the magazine cover again and gives it a wink.

I love Cheryl.

chapter 8

I text Shauna and invite her over to make a vision board. A vision board is a collage of images printed or cut out of magazines and artfully glued on card stock to represent your wishes and goals. Shauna's mom makes them for her work all the time and showed us how. I don't know if it's magic or brain science or karma or what, but supposedly, making a vision board is step one in achieving your dreams. I've never had a bigger wish or goal than I do right now. Plus, collaging is one of my favorite hobbies, even minus the wishes and goals.

> **Shauna:** I'll be right there. I'm learning how to play piano on YouTube.
> **Me:** Srsly?
> **Shauna:** I can almost play "Love Dream" by Franz Liszt. That's legit classical music.
> **Me:** I was gonna say we should duet, but all I can play is "Three Blind Mice." Come over when you're done. Bring gel pens, please.
> **Shauna:** k

When Shauna arrives, I show her my letter. A real letter, not a pretend letter in my RC notebook. It's a little risky embarrassment-wise, but Shauna has been my friend since second grade so I'm not worried. She loves Rory too, and she would never think I'm weird.

Dear Rory,

My name is Millie Jackson, and I go to Susan B. Anthony Middle School, which is near Minneapolis, Minnesota. I have been a fan of yours since my friend Shauna showed me a clip of one of your concerts. Then I saw you featured in *TeenTalk Weekly*, and then I saw the video for the song "Move Me, Girl." And now I must give you congratulations on the success of your hit "Worldwide Crush." It certainly seems to be making a splash with people around the world, especially since you admitted that you are open to sharing your life with a special person from the audience. I wish you great luck with that endeavor. Perhaps you will find them here in my hometown, if you should choose to visit someday. I don't know who that would be, but you never know, as they say.

My best regards to you in your work and your life,
Millie Jackson

"I don't know," she says after reading it. She sits on my floor, leaning against my bed, while I watch her from the bean-bag chair in the corner. We take turns with the beanbag chair. "I mean, I think it's really good—like, extremely professional."

"That's good, right?" I ask. "I don't want to sound like

a dumb kid with a stupid crush." I was trying really hard not to sound like a dumb kid with a stupid crush.

"Well, that's true. You don't sound like a dumb kid. More like an English teacher. Or maybe an accountant. And although that shows great skill, I'm not sure if that's a completely good thing. Like maybe not super *alluring*." When she says "alluring" she makes this flourish with her hand, almost like she's drawing the word out of her mouth with her fingers.

"An accountant?" I say. "I sound like an accountant?"

"Well, kind of." I can tell that Shauna is trying to be kind while telling me my letter sucks. "Unless you think that's what he wants."

I shift uncomfortably in my beanbag. Shauna has a history of challenging me to do things that make me a little uncomfortable. This could be one of those times.

"Millie, you have to think about why you're doing this. Is it just to inform him of your existence on the planet?" She pulls her legs in so she can sit crisscross applesauce and leans forward. "Or do you *want* something? Like a concert, maybe? You barely even mention a concert."

"Yeah, that's a good question," I say, looking down, thinking. "Well, yes, I want him to do a concert here."

"And what else?"

"What else?"

"Yes. What do you *really* want?"

"Well . . . I don't know . . . What else is there?"

"You want him to fall in love with you!"

"*No!* Oh my God, what?! That's crazy! No! How would he fall in love with me from a letter?"

"So you don't want him to fall in love with you?"

"No!"

"You don't?" Shauna squints at me skeptically.

I grab a pencil off the floor and nervously start doodling on a Target receipt I found under my bed.

"Millie, you have to be okay with the fact that you want him to love you, even if that's never going to happen. You know what I mean? Your feelings are your feelings, and you shouldn't let rational thought rob you of that."

"Cripes, Shauna, you sound like my mom. It's like she hired you to be my therapist or something." I throw my pencil at her.

"But I'm right, and you know it." She throws the pencil back at me.

"Maybe we should do something else right now," I say, standing up and looking out my window. "Do you want to ride bikes to the bakery?"

"Nice try, Millie, but no." She's off the floor and grabbing stuff out of my desk—paper, pens, glue stick. "And maybe you should put your picture in the letter."

"What?! I'm just writing him a letter of appreciation, not proposing marriage. He'll think I'm a lunatic."

Her hands full of writing things fall to her sides, and she turns to look at me, her head cocked to the side. "A letter of appreciation? Really? You *appreciate* Rory Calhoun? I'll make sure to put that in my wedding vows."

She walks over and grabs my shoulders, guides me to my desk, pulls out the chair, and pushes me down into it. "You need to be honest with yourself, Millie—you love Rory Calhoun, and wouldn't it be great if he loved you back? Even for the one minute that he reads your letter? I bet tons of people send him pictures. I bet most people do it. Then I think we should do a little research before sending this off. I'm sure we can ask the Google about how to write an effective fan letter."

Shauna was an early adopter of "ask the Google." When we were little, she asked Cheryl how moms got pregnant, and without even looking up from her magazine, Cheryl said, "How should I know, darling? Go ask the Google."

"Fine," I say. "I love him. Let's try."

Shauna smiles and produces her phone from her pocket, and here's what we find out:

....

Six Tips for Writing a Fan Letter That Will Really Get You Noticed

1. **Handwrite your letter:** Handwriting is intensely personal and conveys more emotion. Email is for work and school!

2. **Tell them what you like about them:** But don't do more than a few sentences, because you might sound like a stalker.

3. **Don't say shallow things like "You're so hot!"** It gets old. Make your comments specific and meaningful, like "The way you sing is so amazing." Or "Your eyes are really beautiful and remind me of the ocean." Also, don't ask them to marry you or come to your house. This is probably not going to happen.

4. **Try to show a connection between the two of you:** Do you have something in common? It can be anything from a love of dogs to a favorite color. Your crush will be immediately attracted to you!

5. **Include a picture or a drawing:** Are you a good artist? Draw a picture of a rainbow or something nice. Give them something to make them happy as they go through their day.

6. Ask for what you want: At the very least, ask for an autograph. Many letters don't get replies. But this gives them something quick and easy to give back to you.

That's it! Write your letter! Good luck!

Letter #2

Dear Rory,

My name is Millie Jackson, and I go to Susan B. Anthony Middle School near Minneapolis, Minnesota. I just wanted to tell you that I really enjoy your work, and I think that you are adorable. When I listen to your songs, I feel like I really understand you, and when I watch your videos, I feel like you may be one of the most talented performers ever. I hope you keep doing this forever, and I hope that we can meet someday. I feel like we might have a lot in common, so we could probably talk about a lot of stuff.

For instance, your beloved dog, Sgt. Pepper, who just died, was a bulldog, and my dog, Pringles, is also a bulldog. I'm so sorry about Sgt. Pepper, and I hope your heart stops hurting soon. I think I know how you feel because I love Pringles so much. If there's anything I can do for you, please let me know (Pringles sends slobbery kisses).

I also love the color aquamarine and hope to repaint my bedroom soon in that lovely shade.

So there are two things we have in common, but I'm sure there are more.

I've also been listening to "Worldwide Crush" quite a bit lately, and I think this is my favorite part:

How far must I go just to see your pretty face?

I'll cross the mountains and the deserts to find you . . .

No distance is too far for my heart to find its place . . . in your arms . . . where I belong.

I think that's just beautiful and that you must be some kind of poet, a very talented poet. If I were in your audience listening to those words, I would feel like you were looking for me. Who knows, perhaps you are. ☺ So, as you can see, your words are very powerful.

I have a few questions for you. Where did you grow up? Will you get another dog someday? And, most importantly, will you be coming to Minneapolis on your concert tour? I think you would really like it here. There are tons of lakes, and the hotels are really nice. I think every seventh grader in the state of Minnesota would buy a ticket to your show—possibly seventh graders in Iowa and Wisconsin too. There are so many people here who love you, it would sell out for sure! And my dream would be to sit in the front row. ☺ Please consider us. We would be positively, supremely, and exceedingly grateful!

Well, on that note, I think I will say goodbye and thank you. Thank you for being who you are—so kind and funny—and thank you also for the music and the videos that you give to all of us. I would also like to thank you for having such a cute face, but I know you don't have much to do with that. Ha ha!

Much love and affection,

Millie Jackson

P.S. Please write back if you can. I know you probably can't, but if you can, I would be very grateful. And maybe an autograph! Thanks!

"Awesome," Shauna says.

We fold it and put it in an envelope decorated with bull-dog stickers. Shauna asked the Google about the address, and Cheryl has left me a stamp.

"Where does it go?" I ask, peeling the stamp off its paper and holding it over the envelope.

"Just anywhere, I think," Shauna says, waving her hand over the envelope.

"Really? Maybe I should put it on the back where it's not so crowded." I turn the envelope over, looking for the perfect spot.

"Oh yeah! The stamp is probably for sealing the envelope!"

"We only have one stamp, so maybe I should ask Cheryl so we don't waste this one."

I snap a picture of my fingers holding the stamp over the envelope flap and text it to Cheryl with the word "Here?"

Cheryl texts back a laughing emoji.

Then she tells me that I am "a hoot" and she can't wait to show this picture to the girls at poker. Apparently, the stamp goes in the upper right-hand corner of the envelope, and it has nothing to do with sealing the envelope. And tell me how, exactly, am I supposed to know this?

So we fix the stamp and then drop the letter in the mailbox by the bus stop, which is very exciting because I've been looking at that thing for years without knowing what the heck it was. Shauna does the actual dropping because I'm too nervous; I keep holding it over the open space and then pulling it back, chickening out. Finally, she grabs it from my hand and lets it fall into the darkness, completely out of my control and on its way to Rory Calhoun.

chapter 9

There's a Rory Calhoun concert somewhere in the world every single day. And after each concert, late into the night and way after bedtime, I grab my phone and sneak it under the covers to watch him sing "Worldwide Crush" to that night's chosen person.

Logic says that watching him potentially fall in love with someone that is not me would make me mad and jealous—but it doesn't. It makes me feel the twinge even more. He's so tender with these people, so gentle, totally caring about their nervousness and their tears and looking right into their eyes like, *Hey, it's okay. I'm right here.*

It's like watching what it would be like to be loved by him. And instead of getting jealous, I crush on him even harder.

The first few nights, I cried when I watched him sing to the "Worldwide Crush" people. It's the biggest moment of their lives, and the feelings just pile up and overflow, and they have to spill out. Love makes you cry. It just does. But then I realized that 100 percent of them cried so hard that they looked like tiny babies who got poked with a pin—red, squinchy faces, all wet and splotchy. This is not the time to be ugly! It seems like it would be a better idea to remain as attractive as possible while still being modest and sincere and grateful and loving in return. Right?

Dear RC,

If I were the "Worldwide Crush" girl, I would be flattered but modest, looking up at you coyly from behind the veil of bangs that obscures my humble face. When you sing the words "Is it you who's gonna make me feel alright?" I would put my hand on my chest and close my eyes like, *Wow, this is really happening!* Then I would open my eyes (hand still on chest) and lock eyes with you. Then—this is a really risky move, but I think it would be worth it—I would remove my hand from my chest and hold it out. Not limp and desperate like, *Please, please hold my hand,* but strong and purposeful, like I know you're going to take my hand in yours. And when you do, you will walk closer and stand right in front of me, singing right into my heart. And we stay like that until the end of the song.

    I give your hand a squeeze. Then you lean forward . . . and kiss me gently on the cheek, staying there just a moment so our cheeks hug.

    Then we get married, go on a honeymoon, travel the world together, and you make me waffles every morning. Because that's what you do when you love someone. Hee-hee!

Love and stuff,
Millie

chapter 10

"*Good morning, Jackson family!* Waffles are ready!"
My dad calls us to the table from his post at the stove, peeling
waffles from the iron and stacking them high on a plate. I
come down the stairs and see my mom giving him a kiss on the
cheek as she helps herself to a couple. He pats her butt over her
fuzzy robe with his one free hand, which must mean, "You're
welcome." They think I don't see that stuff, but I totally do.

"Good morning, Millie!" my dad says as I walk into
the room, handing me a plate. "Your lover boy arrived in
the mail this morning."

"What?" What is he talking about?

He grabs a magazine sitting on the counter and cradles it
in his arm, lightly petting the cover and making pretend swoony
lovesick eyes. Then he straightens up, hands it to me, and says,
"When was the last time this kid *wasn't* on the cover?"

It's the new *TeenTalk Weekly*! With Rory on the cover!
Again! God, *look* at him! I grab it quickly and sit down
without even getting my waffle.

"Karl, leave her alone," my mom says as she sits down
next to me with her waffle. "He's adorable; of course they're
going to put him on the cover every week. You can't waste

that face." She sips her coffee with both hands while eyeing the cover. She doesn't hear my dad when he responds, like he's not talking just two feet away from her.

"Didn't she just get one of these things?" She still doesn't look up. "What's up with that? Carrie? What's up with that?"

"It's weekly, Dad. It's right in the title. *TeenTalk Weekly*."

"I don't know; it feels like every day to me."

I wish it were every day. That would be my fantasy. On the cover, just beneath his beautiful chin with absolutely no zits on it, are the words "Get the Stats on Rory Calhoun! (page 26)." Stats! I love stats! I immediately flip to page 26 and start reading.

Cheryl comes in and starts reading over my shoulder. "I think it's funny," she says, "that you still get a paper magazine when you can get all your information from the Google. Isn't this boy on the Facebook? Or the Flooter?"

"It's Flutter," I say.

"That's what I said. Doesn't this boy Flit?"

I don't look up—I'm too busy reading. So my mom answers. "Take a look in her room, Cheryl. It's about the posters. You can't put a Flutter post on your wall."

"Well, you can," says my dad, "but it's not as cute."

Ha. He thinks he's so funny.

....

Get the Stats on Rory Calhoun!

Rory Calhoun fills out our questionnaire with need-to-know info!

Full Name: Rory John Calhoun
Age: 15
Birthday: August 26 (I'm a Virgo!)

Hometown: Bodega Bay, California
Height: 5' 8" (so far)
Hair Color: Sandy blond (blonder in summer)
Eyes: Blue
Favorite Movie: *Sing Street*—a sleeper hit about a boy in 1980s Ireland who starts a band to impress a girl he has a crush on. I love '80s movies.
Favorite Book: *The Hobbit*
Favorite Song: "Let It Be" by the Beatles. It's the first song I learned to play on the guitar.
Favorite Boredom Buster: Yahtzee. It's a total grandma game, but I'm addicted. I have apps on my phone and my laptop, and I have the real deal in a box at home and on the tour bus.
Favorite Snack: I love Funyuns. And when I'm at home, it's BBQ'd oysters. No joke—it's a specialty where I come from.
Favorite Soda: Pibb
Piercings: I have a diamond stud in one ear. I bought my mom some diamond earrings, and she put one in her ear and one in mine. I wear it to remind myself of everything she's done for me.
Favorite Exercise: I'm 15; I don't exercise. But I rehearse a lot, and when I'm home, I surf and walk on the beach.
Favorite Vacation Spot: Home

Dear RC,

Note to self: Go to the library today and get *The Hobbit*.

Love,
Millie

Dear RC,

Note to self: *The Hobbit* is super boring. I don't think I can finish it. I've started it three times, and I keep having to start over because I forget what happened. Or I'll be reading and suddenly realize I'm thinking about something else, like how Carson wet his pants in gym in second grade. I don't even know if I could tell you what this book is about, even though I'm on page 136. I think there's a dragon? Some small people? That may not even be right, I could've gotten that from the movie. So maybe Rory and I won't be able to talk about *The Hobbit*, but I still think it's cute that he likes this totally confusing book.

Love,
Millie

Dear RC,

Note to self: And also, ask the Google about Bodega Bay, California.

Love,
Millie

chapter 11

After school, I go to Target with my mom for a new binder because she bought me a one-inch binder for language arts when she was supposed to buy a one-and-a-half-inch binder. And now I walk around with a binder that doesn't close and crumpled papers poking out and falling on the ground. I even hand in my homework all wrinkled. I'm like a seventh-grade boy. How do boys live like that? And also, Billy got the wrong kind of crayons, which won't wash off walls. My mom is not super happy right now.

As we approach the toy section, I realize we're walking right by without stopping . . . like it doesn't even apply to me anymore. When was the last time I begged my mom to stop in the toy section? When was the last time I got a toy for a gift? Was it the Playmobil family motor home? With foldable table and rooftop storage? How long ago was that? And for a moment, I'm just a little bit sad, remembering all the good times I had with the Playmobil family motor home. I miss you, Target toy section.

The last endcap in the toy section has a display of board games—old-school games packaged like they were in the olden days when my parents played games. I see Yahtzee. And my hand reaches out and touches it as if Rory Calhoun himself touched this game. I grab it and chase after my mom who is already around the corner in the lawn and garden section. When I meet up with her, I'm totally cool, like I totally don't care, and I casually toss the Yahtzee game into our cart, like it's a box of saltine crackers or something. Ho hum.

She stops walking. "What's that?"

"It's a game." I refrain from saying "duh."

She stares at it. "No, it's not. Where's the screen?"

"Ha ha. I just thought it might be nice to have family game night sometime."

She shifts her weight to her other foot, both hands still on the cart, and eyes me with suspicion. "Who *are* you?" she says.

"Whatever. I'll put it back." I reach into the cart and grab the box.

"No!" She reaches out to stop me and puts the game back in the cart. "I like it. I just hope this isn't some preteen conspiracy to take over the world while their parents are absorbed in eighties-era board games." She starts walking again. "Bring on the family game night, sister."

After we get home, I take the Yahtzee to my room and put it on the shelf across from my bed so I can look at it tonight while I'm falling asleep. Then I dig around in my closet for my Playmobil family motor home. I just want to look at it and maybe move the pieces around a little bit. You know, for old time's sake.

I find it parked on a low shelf way off to the left, behind a shoebox full of Easter candy—oh Schmidt, how long has that been there? The whole family is inside, thrown about like they were in a very catastrophic motor home accident. Poor family. I carefully place each one upright, Mom's hands on the wheel. I look over my shoulder before I drive them around on the carpet, just for a minute, quickly, before someone sees me.

I wonder where they should go?

Hmmm . . . how about Bodega Bay, California?

chapter 12

@minneapolismayor @millieluvsbulldogs
Thank you for contacting the mayor of Minneapolis! Your comment is important to us! Let's work hard to make Minneapolis amazing . . . *together*!

What?! What the cheeseball does that even mean, anyway?

chapter 13

The next day, during outdoor free-choice time, I pull out my phone and tap "Bodega Bay" into the search bar. We are allowed to use our electronic devices during outdoor free-choice time—otherwise they have to stay in our lockers, because they are a distraction. I have to agree with the teachers on this one; how can Mr. Sneed talking about integers be more interesting than a video of a baby otter eating a carrot?

Shauna is spending her outdoor free-choice time in the library because she likes to help Darius, the library specialist, shelve books. She says the outdoor part of outdoor free-choice time is not a good fit for her. I like to shelve books too, but today I have some private research to do. I've been thinking and dreaming about Bodega Bay all day. It sounds so romantic—*Bodega Bay*—and not just romantic in a kissy way but more like a dramatic way, like maybe it would be the setting of a mystery book or something. *Bodega Bay* . . .

I wait for the results to load while I sit on a bench facing the climbing apparatus, which is middle school speak for "jungle gym." You wouldn't think a middle school would still need playground equipment, but it's clearly necessary for a certain segment of the seventh and eighth grade population. The boys hang on the climbing apparatus like monkeys while the girls walk the perimeter of the playground, deep in conversation. The boys are like preschoolers, and the girls are like old ladies. Unless you're one of the sporty girls playing sports—they look like professional athletes. Or Carson and Hawthorne, who look like they're rehearsing a scene from *Star Wars*.

My phone is super old, so it takes a long time to load stuff. Gob! I could just kill my parents for this injustice. They feel strongly that a phone is "only a communication device intended for your safety and security, rather than a form of entertainment." Therefore, someone's stupid leftover phone is all I need. Honestly, I believe they think suffering will make me a better person.

Finally, the search results pop up, and the first link is the website for the city of Bodega Bay:

Bodega Bay, California:
Rugged Beaches and Whale Watching
near Sonoma Valley Wineries.

Rugged beaches! Whale watching! Wine! Okay, I don't care about wine that much, but my mom sure does. The rest sounds totally dramatic and romantic—dramantic?—just like I thought.

This stretch of the Sonoma Coast—about an hour and a half north of San Francisco—is an ideal spot for strolling, fishing, and spotting a variety of unusual birds, especially within the Sonoma Coast State Beaches. One of the best views of the rugged seascape can be found at Bodega Head, a craggy beachfront cliff located just outside town.

Dramantic! It sounds like the place where the lovers in the book would meet—or where the murder takes place.

This coastal region also produces some of the Pacific Ocean's tastiest oysters. A half-hour drive down the coastal highway will take you to Tomales Bay Oyster Company, where locals slurp down raw shellfish at waterside picnic tables.

Gross. No, thank you. Is there something else I can slurp at the waterside picnic tables?

The outdoor scenes in the Alfred Hitchcock–directed film *The Birds* (1963) were filmed in Bodega Bay. Other movies filmed in or around Bodega Bay include *The Goonies; The Russians Are Coming, the Russians Are Coming*; and *Summer of '42*.

The Goonies! I totally know that movie! The others, I have no idea. Question: Why do they film so many movies there? Is it because of its vacation-like beauty?

Click here for Chowder Day results.

I love chowder!

The epic annual migration of gray whales from Northern Alaska to the lagoons off the Baja Peninsula of Mexico is visible January through April. A great vantage point is the ocean overlook at Bodega Head and the whale-watching trips in the local area. . . .

Hmm. Do I like whales? I think I do. Is that considered Earth science? Whales are also dramantic.

Bucolic scenery of cattle and sheep farms. Hills are green in May; wildflowers are in full bloom. Rolling grass-covered hills and stands of cypress trees along the shore. You may be shrouded in fog, blasted by wind, or bathed in sunny skies.

Seriously, this sounds made up by some famous author. And it certainly doesn't sound like the California they show on TV; I never pictured cows and sheep in Hollywood.

Shark attack season is August through November.

Gob! Ignoring this, although it's still pretty dramantic. Maybe one of the lovers falls off the rugged cliff into the ocean, and the other lover dives in to save her only to get eaten by a shark. The end.

Dear RC,

Bodega Bay seems *beautiful*, with rocky cliffs and crashing ocean waves and sheep and cows. I have never seen the ocean before, as our vacations are spent at either a Wisconsin Dells water park or at my great-grandma's condo in Phoenix. (It is free. That's why we go there. We don't go there in the summertime, though, because it is H-O-T.) Sometimes we go other places, but it's always driving, like to the world's tallest statue of Paul Bunyan.

None of these things are that interesting to me anymore. Truthfully, they weren't that interesting to me at the time either, but I enjoyed eating fast food on the road and swimming in hotel pools, so I didn't really complain.

Instead, I would like to go someplace like Bodega Bay so I can see the ocean and see how a place like that turned you into the person you are: nice, tan, outdoorsy, sensitive, and sweet, with honey-blond hair blowing in the wind.

Now I can see that a lot of your love songs talk about the ocean:

"Hold my hand, let's leave footprints in the sand."

"The waves of your love keep crashing against my heart."

And I bet when you say, "You lift me higher than the birds," you're actually referencing that Alfred Hitchbomb (whatever his name is) movie about birds. Except that it's a horror movie, and you probably wouldn't reference a horror movie in a love song. Either way, I know what you mean now, and I think it's really romantic. You probably can't help it, because the place where you live is so romantic.

I'm pretty sure there are no love songs inspired by the Wisconsin Dells or the world's tallest statue of Paul Bunyan. And the way things are looking, the mayor of Minneapolis is not going to offer you a key to the city made out of pizza. In general, Minnesota is not working for me right now.

Perhaps Bodega Bay would be a better fit.

Love and stuff,
Millie

P.S. Check airfares to California tonight.

P.P.S. Oh my Gawd, that's a lot of money. Is that how much a regular airline ticket would be? I thought it would be like a hundred bucks. This is more like a whole week of veterinarian camp. I know this because two summers ago, I begged my parents to sign me up for veterinarian camp, and it was a big decision because it was very expensive. Turned out to be more cow oriented than I expected—I thought I'd be taking care of pandas and stuff. Ask the Google about places to stay anyway, even if it costs more than veterinarian camp.

chapter 14

Just checked my mailbox for a letter from Rory Calhoun. No reply yet. Is it unrealistic to be checking my mailbox so soon? Yes—the answer is yes. My logical brain knows that the answer is yes. The laws of math and science make it impossible for my letter to have been picked up, put on a truck, then put on a plane, then put on another truck, then delivered to Rory, then opened and read (where he sees my picture and immediately falls in love with me. Ha ha! Just kidding!) in this amount of time.

Then you have to allot time for him to write a proper response. That could take some time. And when he's done, he will put it in an envelope and lick the flap to seal it—oh my God! When I get my letter, will it have Rory Calhoun's spit on it? I never thought of that!—then picked up, put on a truck, put on a plane, put on another truck, and delivered to my house (where I open it, read it, and say, "Yes, I'll marry you!" Ha ha again!).

In other words, that's a lot of days. But I keep checking anyway, just in case.

In the meantime, I dream about Bodega Bay and check Flutter for any notifications.

@stpaulmayor @millieluvsbulldogs
The Office of the Mayor of St. Paul is here for you! Your comment or suggestion will help make this city great! We will get to it as soon as we can!

Poo.

chapter 15

Instead of straight up asking if we can take an expensive vacation to an unknown small town in California, I decide to subtly and slowly provide my parents with information that might lead them to come up with that fantastic idea on their own.

I start by talking about my lifelong love of whales at the dinner table. (Not that I love whales *at the dinner table* but that I *bring it up* at the dinner table. Sheesh, you know what I mean.) I feel like parents are much more likely to listen to you and do what you want if you talk about things that are educational. If you just talk about things you want, they start singing that Rolling Stones song called "You Can't Always Get What You Want." As if I should know this song as anything other than a song that parents sing to kids who ask for stuff.

So maybe if I focus on whales and nature and my future as a potential marine biologist, they will listen instead of singing that dumb song.

So at dinner I wait for a lull in the conversation, and then I blurt out, "One thing I regret in my lifetime is that I've never experienced the whale migration off the coast of Northern California."

Everyone stops chewing and stares at me.

I stare back. "I mean . . . because . . . whales . . ."

Perhaps I should've practiced this.

They're still staring at me, not chewing.

"I really love whales." I say it quietly, like I'm confessing a dirty secret.

"Whales?" my dad says.

"Yes."

"You love whales?" my mom asks, confused.

"Mm-hmm. I can't believe you didn't know that." That'll make them feel like bad parents. I hope, anyway.

My mom and dad look at each other.

"Since when?" my mom asks.

"Since always."

"Huh. I had no idea." She takes a bite of her sandwich. It's sandwich night. My mom's is tuna.

"Right. I know. I've been keeping it kind of a secret . . ." Oops. I just scolded them for not knowing, and now it's a secret? I'm not good at lying.

"So you *secretly* love whales?" my dad says.

"Yes, well, I didn't know how you would feel about it . . ."

"About you liking whales?" My mom's face is a combination of confusion and amusement.

This is not going how I planned.

"Yes, because one time, a long time ago, I overheard you saying something about whales and how the Save the Whales people were crazy, so I was worried that you would think I was a Save the Whales person."

That's a total lie. I lifted it from our discussion about activist movements in social studies.

"What? I never said that." My mom looks around at the other people at the dinner table. "Why would I say that? What's wrong with Save the Whales people?"

"Maybe it wasn't you. Maybe it was someone else, and I just thought it was you. But either way, I can't keep it inside any longer."

"It could've been me," says Cheryl. She has peanut butter, like Billy. "I think anyone who comes to my door with a clipboard, asking for money, is a pain in the ass."

"Well," I say, trying to be confident, "I just really love whales, and I'm worried that my whole life will go by without achieving my lifelong dream of seeing the whale migration off the coast of Northern California."

"Well," my mom says, "that sounds serious. We can't have you dying without achieving your lifelong dream." She grabs a potato chip—we have chips on sandwich night— between her thumb and forefinger and shoves it in her mouth, keeping her eyes on me. I can't tell if she's making fun of me or not. I think she is.

"I don't hate whales," says Cheryl. "I just hate people coming to my door asking for money. It's nothing personal between the whales and me."

This didn't go well. I'll have to make another plan for tomorrow.

Dear RC,

My coonskin hat came today! Yay! Let's see if it makes me sexy (wink wink)! I will start by wearing it just in the house. When it feels natural, I will wear it around my yard only, then I will branch out into the neighborhood, then the bus stop, and finally on the bus. I'm not allowed to wear it in school because they're afraid we'll share hats and give each other lice.

Love and stuff,
Millie

Dear RC,

I only made it to the backyard phase of my coonskin-hat experiment. After just one day, the tail part of the hat got chewed off by the neighbor's dog, Pickles. Stupid Pickles. Now it looks like one of those furry Russian hats.

    Gob!

Love,
Millie

chapter 16

Today in the lunchroom, Shauna puts down her milk carton and says, "What's going on over there?" She's looking over at The Blondes: Trinity Breen, Taylor Hanson, Leaf Garrett, and Iris Moriarty. They are a super tight group of superfriends, and they are all blonde, as in white blonde. It's like looking at a lunch table for ghosts.

I turn to look. I have a mouthful of gummy fruit, but I stop chewing when I see them—they're all bouncing in their seats and looking at their phones. They look like bunnies who all rolled a Yahtzee. Then they all take their one free hand and high-five each other, not in one slap like normal people do but in many rapid-fire clap-clap-claps. It's like a mega high five that never stops.

This is so weird. Everyone is watching now, wondering what The Blondes find so exciting. Is there a new flavor at the frozen yogurt shop? A sale on lip gloss? What?

That's when I hear their quiet chant, their heads together in a little circle whispering all together—they're saying, "Rory! Rory! Rory!"

Oh my God. "Shauna, get your phone out!"

"You get *your* phone out."

"Mine is in my locker! Do it! Hurry!" I don't take my eyes off The Blondes, who are still group hugging.

Shauna looks at me for a moment and then looks back at The Blondes. When she hears the chant, she drops her bologna sandwich and scrambles for her backpack, finding her phone and pulling it out.

"What do I do?" she says, a little bit panicky.

"Go to his Flutter!"

"Oh my God. Oh my God." It takes all of no seconds for Shauna to open his Flutter (I hate my phone!), and she reaches her hand out for me to grab.

I grab it and say, "What?!"

"Okay—it's nothing for sure yet—but it looks like our time is coming." She turns the phone around to show me the screen, and here is what it says:

@rorycalhoun
Announcing cities for my US tour TODAY! Check here at 3:30 CT to see if your city will be one of our stops!

"Holy Christmas . . . Shauna . . ."

"I know." We look at each other seriously, not sure what to say, stunned by the possibility of what could be. But also fully aware that the possibility could slip through our fingers if our city doesn't appear on that list. I think we are also afraid of behaving like The Blondes.

Finally, I speak. "We need to be prepared. On the one hand, this could be a life-changing announcement. On the other hand, it could be the disappointment of a lifetime. And we need to make sure your phone has a full charge at the end of the day so we can check at exactly three thirty."

"We'll be on the bus. I don't know if that's good or bad, but I'm turning my phone off right now to save battery." She holds the button down, and I feel like hugging her—like we're going off to war or something—but instead we just exchange a meaningful nod and get ready to go back to class.

My heart pounds all the way to math. I hear nothing Mr. Sneed says the whole hour. Fifth hour is just as bad. And when I arrive at social studies at the end of the day, Dr. Marion has heard the news. I know this because on the board, in all caps, are the words "RORY CALHOUN." Oh, sigh! Is it possible that today, in social studies, whatever that is, we will talk about Rory Calhoun?! The room is electric. She waits for all of us to sit down, and, when the bell rings, she turns and writes "cultural phenomenon" (really big vocab word) under his beautiful name.

"A cultural phenomenon," she says, "is defined as a fact or an event that influences the behavior of large groups of people and is often difficult to understand or explain fully. In other words, it's something in our culture that makes people go cuckoo. Fashion trends, dance crazes, even some toys are considered phenomena. But what we have with Rory Calhoun is a very special kind of cultural phenomenon. I'll give you another example . . ."

Dr. Marion mentions a boy band from the nineties called the Backstreet Boys, specifically the one named Howie, who "inspired a unique hysteria among a particular population." She says young people all over the world fell in love with the Backstreet Boys, especially Howie. She really makes it seem like Howie is the most important Backstreet Boy. She turns and writes the words "Howie," "teen idol," and "celebrity crush" on the board.

"If you'd like some extra-credit homework, you can look up definitions for the terms 'teen idol' and 'celebrity crush' and give me one paragraph on how our culture has been influenced by Rory Calhoun."

Then she offers to answer any questions we may have about the Backstreet Boys or Howie—especially Howie. She starts to erase the board, but when she gets to Rory's name, she turns and smiles at us and says, "And good luck to you all at three thirty today. My fingers will be crossed for you."

I think Dr. Marion has a celebrity crush. And for a fleeting moment, I dare to wonder if I will still love Rory Calhoun when I am old.

chapter 17

At 3:25 p.m., every girl on the bus has her phone out, staring at the screen waiting. We refresh, refresh, refresh, just in case he posts something early. And then, at exactly 3:30 p.m. and some seconds, a moment of silence. Seriously, there is absolutely no sound on the bus except for that boy making fart noises with his armpit. And then, as if directed by Ms. Burson, the choir teacher, we all suck in a giant breath . . .

And let it out slowly, like a deflating balloon.

I see New York. I see Chicago. I see Atlanta. And Detroit. I don't see Minneapolis.

I read the whole list again, just in case I missed it. But it's not there . . . he's not coming.

I turn and look out the window, unable to think of anything to say. And in the glass, I see the reflection of everyone else whose world just ended.

Dear RC,

Do you know how it feels
After the one thing you want is stolen by Detroit?
My heart hurts.
My future is broken.
I can't eat dinner.
Tonight sucks.

Bereft (vocab word meaning "robbed of"),
Millie

My phone dings while I lie on my bed, staring at the ceiling. If it's not Shauna, or Rory Calhoun himself telling me he's changed his mind, I'm going to ignore it.

> **Shauna:** What about Chicago?
> **Me:** What about it?
> **Shauna:** Why can't we go to Chicago for the concert?
> **Me:** Because we're not millionaires?
> **Shauna:** Seriously. My mom met her sisters there to see *Hamilton*, and she was only gone for one night. Rory Calhoun is way bigger than Alexander Hamilton.

I sit up slowly, hope creeping back into my body. Could this work? Together we ask the Google, use our calculators, and send rapid-fire texts back and forth to see if this could actually happen.

> **Me:** Distance between Minneapolis and Chicago is 408 miles.
> **Shauna:** It would take 5.82 hours to drive there.
> **Me:** We didn't even drive that far when my mom's uncle Jesse died this summer. We just sent flowers.

Shauna: What about flying?

Me: Looks like it takes one and a half hours. But I only have $137 in my bank account.

Shauna: Plus, we would need to stay in a hotel overnight.

Me: And if the concert is on a school night, we would have to skip school. And one of our parents would have to take at least two days off of work.

Shauna: That's basically like asking for a trip to Disney World. Hold on. I'm asking anyway.

Shauna: My mom said "maybe someday." Which means no.

I don't reply because I feel robbed again.

Shauna: I'm sorry, Millie.

Me: I'm sorry too. It was a good idea.

Shauna: Luv u.

Me: Luv u 2.

I bury myself in acrostic poems and collages. I don't want to talk to anyone—not even Cheryl. I just want to be by myself in my room. I scan the Internet for pictures of Rory Calhoun and whales and print them out. I'm sitting on the floor of my room, cutting out freshly printed whale photos, when I hear: "Hey! Who used up all the ink?! These were brand-new cartridges!" This is followed by footsteps up the stairs, followed by my dad standing in the doorway of my room looking down at me on the floor, surrounded by fresh printouts.

I look up at him, scissors in one hand, whale photo in the other, and give him an "oopsie" face. Hopefully, that's enough to keep him from getting too mad.

"Millie, what the heck is this? This has gotta be twenty full-color photos."

"I'm . . . sorry. I'm making a collage."

"Of whales?" He kneels down and picks up some of the photos and looks at them. "Wow. Look at this one." He holds out a black-and-white photo of a whale tail, backlit by the sun.

"I know," I say. "And look at this one. This one is my favorite."

He takes it from my hand and looks at it—and smiles. "Well, they certainly are majestic animals, aren't they? I can see why you like them."

But my sad face makes him concerned. "Are you okay, honey?"

"Yes," I lie. "I'm fine."

Dear RC,

Wondrous,

Highly intelligent,

Amazing,

Lives in liquid.

Eyes can view them from Bodega Bay, California.

Someday I will see one.

Love,

Millie

I rip it out of my notebook. This goes on the inside of my bedroom door, right next to a photo of Rory looking out to sea.

chapter 18

When tickets go on sale in Chicago, I casually check online to see how much tickets are, just in case. I know Shauna's mom said, "Maybe someday," but what if she really meant maybe someday? What if we're wrong, and our parents would gladly buy plane tickets and let us skip school for this once-in-a-lifetime cultural experience?

But it doesn't matter how much they are, because it's sold out. Tickets went on sale this morning, and by the time school is out, they're gone.

I check Atlanta and Detroit and Philadelphia and Schenectady, even though I don't know where that is—sold out. It's all sold out, everywhere. Even if I owned a private jet, I still couldn't go to a Rory Calhoun concert. It feels like getting robbed a third time.

Maybe this is not meant to be. Maybe I'm too young to understand how this works, or too not rich, or too suburban, or too something else. Maybe this is not for people like me—whatever that is. I just wish I knew what it is I'm supposed to be.

I stop daydreaming about concerts. And I start daydreaming about Bodega Bay. If I can't see Rory in concert, I can still look for him in other places. I can find the essence of Rory, feel his Roryness, in the place where he became Rory Calhoun. And maybe I'll meet a local shopkeeper who will think, *Wow, this girl would be perfect for Rory; maybe I'll call him up and just let him know.* And Rory would fly home, just for the day, and we would run into each other at the deli or the bookstore, and he would see what sandwich I ordered or what book I was reading. And he'd be like, "Hey, that's *my* favorite sandwich!" Or, "Hey, that's what *I'm* reading!" As long as it's not *The Hobbit*, of course. And then he'd know—this is the girl.

So I try one more time to turn the dinnertime conversation toward Bodega Bay. This time, I've memorized important facts about whale migration, and, most importantly, I will introduce Bodega Bay as a vacation spot.

Tonight is takeout night, so I wait until everyone has grabbed their chicken out of the bucket. Billy likes the ones with "handles," so I dig around for some chicken legs for him. I try to wait an adequate amount of time, give people a chance to enjoy their food, before I begin.

"Billy," my mom says, "you have to eat the meat that's underneath the crust. You can't just eat the crust."

Billy's plate is full of beautifully skinned chicken legs. Billy looks at my mom and then down at his naked chicken legs. He lightly touches the smooth meat of one piece with his tiny pointer finger. "I don't want to," he says.

"But honey, that's the food part, where the nutrition is."

"I don't want nutrition," he says.

That's when I blurt out: "The epic annual migration of gray whales from the Chukchi Sea off Northern Alaska to the lagoons off the Baja Peninsula of Mexico is visible

January through April. A great vantage point is the ocean overlook at Bodega Head in Bodega Bay, California, and the whale-watching trips in the local area—"

"Did you say 'Ba-*ja*'?" my dad interrupts, with a hard *j* sound.

I actually have a lot more memorized. "Um, I think so. It's a peninsula. Where whales go."

"He's teasing, honey," my mom says. "It's pronounced 'Ba-*ha*.'"

"Oh. Ba-ha. Yeah, I know," I lie. "It's just that some people say 'Ba-*ja*,' so, you know. . ."

"Who says 'Ba-ja'?" my dad says. He's a little indignant, like, *Who would say that?!*

"Oh whatever, Karl. Stop bugging her. Go on, sweetheart." My mom picks up her chicken handle and takes a bite.

Now I've lost my train of thought. "Well . . . so . . . Bodega Bay, California, seems to be one of the best places to see whales. You know, if that's your thing." I'm trying to be casual so it doesn't seem like I'm asking for something.

"If that's your thing," my mom says, taking another bite of chicken. Except she says "thang," like she's trying to be the cool mom. It's not working. It's actually making me nervous because it seems like she's not listening.

Cheryl is listening, though. She grabs a napkin and wipes her hands before adding her two cents. "Those Save the Whales people should knock on doors and ask for money there. In . . . what is it?"

"Bodega Bay."

"Bodega Bay," she repeats. "That's where they'll make some real money."

"Yeah, Bodega Bay." I say it again, just so I can plant the seed in everyone's mind.

Dear RC,

I wonder if you've ever seen any whales from Bodega Head? That would be a cool feature to have in your town. We don't have anything like that here. The closest thing we have to something interesting is the giant chicken statue outside the grocery store. And that's not even alive, so I'm not sure it really counts.

For some reason, I like to picture you loving whales. It seems very noble and compassionate. And I already know that you're an animal lover, because of your sadness over the death of your dog, Sgt. Pepper. Just the fact that you had a dog and shared that with all of us shows what an animal lover you are. And then you were brave enough to post about your sadness when he died. I felt so bad for you that day. I think animal lovers have bigger hearts than other people. I can totally see that in your eyes—you have a big heart, and it makes me want to put my lips on your cheek and smell your skin and feel your smile.

But since I can't do that, I will give my dog, Pringles, a big hug for you.

Love for real,
Millie

That night, I tell my mom once again that she doesn't need to tuck me in anymore. But still she comes to my room, tucks the blanket under my chin, and says, "I'm not. I'm just checking on you."

"You just *tucked* the blanket under my chin. That's tucking me in."

"So if I just came in here and did everything the same but I didn't touch the blankets, that would be allowed?"

"I don't know. I guess. Actually, you don't even need to come in here at all. What are you even checking on?"

"Oh, Millie . . . someday you'll understand."

"No, Mom, someday *you'll* understand."

With that, she starts laughing and grabs the blanket and starts tucking it under my chin over and over again. "Just for that, young lady, I'm going to tuck you in like a hundred times! There! How do you like that?!"

"Mom! Stop it!" But I'm totally laughing—something I really haven't done much lately.

She kisses me hard on the cheek, and I turn my head and squeeze my eyes shut so it doesn't look like I'm too happy about it.

"Mom," I say nervously. I don't know why I'm doing this, but she seems happy, and it seems like it might be an okay time, so I just blurt it out: "Mom, do you think we could go to California?"

"Of course, sweetheart," she says, reaching for my lamp to turn it off. "You can go anywhere and do anything you set your mind to. You just have to work hard and believe in yourself."

The lamp goes out, and she turns to give me another kiss, this time on the forehead, and walks out the door.

Holy Christmas.

That could be the most inappropriate use of the "you can do anything" speech I've ever heard. What am I supposed to do, take my allowance to the airport and buy a first-class ticket? It's called listening, Carrie!

I turn on my tiny reading light and grab my RC notebook.

Dear RC,

We never go anywhere.
High up on a waterslide doesn't count.
And Arizona is okay but . . .
Let's live a little,
Escape to someplace new,
See something educational . . . like whales.

Love,
Millie

I think about ripping it out and putting it on the bathroom mirror where my mom and dad will see it. Then I change my mind, and I quietly open my door and tape it next to my whale collage and other acrostic whale poems, making my door a growing tribute to my new favorite animal—a shrine for all to admire as they walk past my room and down the stairs.

Maybe it'll help some people get a clue.

chapter 19

Shauna and I are walking the perimeter at outdoor free-choice time. She wore pigtails yesterday, so today her hair is smooth and wavy. Mine feels like a haystack on my head, which is why I wear it in a ponytail every day. There isn't enough conditioner in all of Target to make my hair look that nice. Shauna tucks a wavy lock behind her ear, like she doesn't even care about her nice hair, and says, "I have some good news. I think . . ."

"You think?"

"Yeah. My mom found a language camp in northern Minnesota that teaches Tagalog."

"What's Tagalog?"

"Millie!" She stops walking to look me in the face. "If you're going to be my friend, you have to know this! It's one of the languages of the Philippines." She turns and starts walking again.

"Eek! I did not know that," I say, trying to catch up with her. "Shauna, this is awesome! Because then you'll feel . . ."

"Like *me*!" She puts her hands over her heart as she walks.

"Yes. Okay, this *is* good news."

"It's a really big deal, actually," she says, talking with her hands, all excited. "People come from all over the country to go to this camp—that's how good it is. And it's two weeks long. And did I mention it's overnight camp and not day camp?"

"Two weeks?!" Now it's my turn to stop walking. "Shauna, that means I'll be by myself this summer for two weeks?"

"Yes, but you'll be fine. Maybe you can hang out with Carson and Hawthorne."

"And do what, play Nerf lightsabers for two weeks?"

"Millie, come on," she says, pulling me forward by the arm. "We're talking about my sense of self versus what games you do or do not like to play. I think you can manage this for me."

"I'm sorry. Yes, for you I will play Nerf lightsabers for two weeks this summer."

"Thank you. Maybe I will be a new, confident woman when I get back."

We walk in silence for a bit, rounding the corner by the basketball hoop. She tucks a wavy lock behind her ear again and points to Devi Jones sitting on the swings. Sitting next to her is Theo from my social studies class.

Boys never go on the swings.

"What do you suppose is going on there?" Shauna says.

"Huh," I say. "Swinging?"

"Do you think they're dating?"

"I don't know. I hate that word—what is dating, anyway?"

"It means you're going on dates."

"To the swings?"

"Maybe. And the bus," Shauna says. "If they're sitting next to each other on the bus, we'll know."

"So what do they *do*? When they're dating?"

"I don't think they *do* anything."

"And people enjoy that?"

"Apparently."

We watch as Devi swings in small arcs, turning to look at Theo occasionally while he talks to her. Sometimes she gives a small smile or a shrug.

"Look at her," I say. "She looks so nonchalant. I would love to be nonchalant."

"Someday you'll be nonchalant, Millie. You're just not there yet."

My phone buzzes in my pocket. When I reach for it, I see that Shauna is reaching for hers too. Across the playground, I see Devi Jones reaching for her phone while she swings. So does Trinity Breen, and Taylor Hanson, and Iris and Amina and Leaf. Every girl on the playground is looking at her phone.

"Millie . . ." Shauna holds her phone up so I can see the screen.

@rorycalhoun
Special concert announcement: Due to popular demand, more cities will be added to US tour. Final cities and dates announced today at 3:30 p.m. via Flutter and rorycalhoun.com.

The energy on the playground turns electric. And I close my eyes and lay my head on Shauna's shoulder, feeling a combination of relief and hope. I've got another shot.

chapter 20

Once again, at 3:25 p.m., every girl on the bus has her phone out, staring at the screen, waiting. We refresh, refresh, refresh, just like last time, in case he posts something early. And again, at exactly 3:30 p.m. and some seconds, a moment of silence. Even the boy who does armpit farts is silent this time. We all suck in one giant breath when the announcement appears on the screen . . . and the bus explodes in a cheer that just about blows the top right off. People stand up and climb over seats to hug each other, and the bus driver yells, "Sit down! Sit down!" but no one pays any attention. Because this is what we see:

....

Special announcement from rorycalhoun.com:

Due to popular demand, Rory Calhoun
will be ADDING the following cities to his
US Worldwide Crush Tour:

Click on your city for concert info.
Tickets go on sale Friday at 10:00 a.m.

Denver, Colorado
Cleveland, Ohio
Portland, Oregon
San Jose, California
Minneapolis, Minnesota

I stop reading after the words "Minneapolis" and "Minnesota." The words "Minneapolis" and "Minnesota" just changed my life. Forever.

We click through for more info, and Shauna takes in a sharp breath.

"Look at the date!" she says. "It's the day before your birthday! Do you know what this means? Millie, this is your birthday party! You could potentially celebrate your birthday at Rory Calhoun!"

In my head, I take it one step further: if I'm the "Worldwide Crush" girl, I could potentially celebrate my birthday *with* Rory Calhoun.

The bus driver is always yelling at us to walk, but today there is nothing he can do—every single girl pushes her way off that bus and takes off running toward home, including me. There's no time for rules today! Shauna and I run side by side until she splits off for her house. "Go!" she says. "You ask your mom, and I'll ask mine! One of them will say yes and take us both . . ."

I watch her running away from me, her backpack bumping on her back, and I call after her, "What if she says no?"

Shauna turns around and runs backward for a little while, her arms pumping. "Don't say that! Think positive! Plus, I could totally buy you a ticket because I have tons of cat-sitting money!" Then she turns and runs for home.

It's possible that my excitement didn't do me any favors. Instead of coming in the house and greeting my mother kindly and then saying, "Dear Mother, I have some wonderful news! In addition to getting an A on my vocab test, I also found out that Rory Calhoun, my favorite person in the whole world besides you, is coming in concert! Isn't that exciting? And I wondered if we could discuss the possibility of going to the concert—after my homework is finished, of course." My approach was more like this: I run inside; slam the door, which I am told repeatedly not to do; throw my backpack on the floor, which I am told repeatedly not to do; run to my mom, who is reading the newspaper, like the real paper kind; and grab the newspaper out of her hand so violently that she jumps and yelps like a puppy. And then she yells at me for being so rude, and while she's yelling, I'm going, "Mom! Mom! Mom! Mom! Mom!"

And finally, I say, "Will you just be quiet and listen to me?!"

Which she did not like—at all.

That's when she looks at me really hard and says, very quietly, "Excuse me?"

Gob! I haven't even begun to ask, and I can already feel it slipping away! I've just never had this kind of request before—I have literally never asked for anything more important, and she holds all the power, sitting there, looking up at me with her angry eyes.

I gently and carefully hand her the newspaper I just grabbed out of her hands while saying, "Sorry, sorry, sorry! It's just that I just found out, right now on the bus, that Rory Calhoun is coming in concert! And I have to go! Shauna is asking her mom right now, this very minute, and I need to know if I can go!"

She takes the newspaper cautiously with one hand and holds the other one up in a "back off" gesture and says,

"Okay, just calm down a bit, Millie, and maybe we can talk about it tonight."

I do not like the "maybe" part. As if this is a casual opportunity, like bowling with my Brownie troop. It makes me feel panicky. "Mom! I need to know right now because I need to call Shauna, and tickets go on sale on Friday, and I just really need to go, I like really, really, really have to go! If I don't go . . . Oh my God, I just have to go! Mom, please! Mom—"

"Millie!" She cuts me off. "I don't appreciate you throwing this at me and demanding an immediate response! I'd be happy to discuss the issue with you rationally, maybe at dinner tonight, but not like this." She gets up and walks toward the kitchen, and I follow. "This is a big deal," she says. "It's your first concert, it costs a lot of money, I have no information about who is involved, how you're getting there, or"—she stops and turns to look at me—"do you expect that I will go and be the chauffeur?"

"Yes! Yes! But it would be awesome, I promise!"

"I don't even know if we're free that night," she says as she puts the newspaper on the mail pile—again, like we're talking about bowling.

"Oh, right," I say. "Like I'm going to be all, 'Sorry, I can't go to this once-in-a-lifetime opportunity because I have Girl Scouts that night.'"

"You haven't been in Girl Scouts for years," she says casually as she looks through the mail.

"Whatever! That's not the point! Mom! Can I go?! Please!"

"Millie!" She slams the mail on the counter. "This is too much! I can't think like this!" She shakes her head and walks away from me, completely unaware that she's shattering my dreams.

My phone dings, and I look down to see a text from Shauna.

Shauna: My mom isn't home, and she isn't answering my texts.

Me: Did not go well here.

Shauna: Piffle! What happened?

Me: I got overly excited and stole her newspaper and told her to be quiet in a not-so-appropriate way.

Shauna: Ouch.

Me: We might talk about it at dinner.

Shauna: Crossing my fingers.

Me: I'm going to rethink my approach. Must be zen.

Shauna: How can you be zen? It's Rory Calhoun. Doesn't she get that?

Me: Definitely not.

Shauna: Has she looked in your room lately? Doesn't she wonder about that kid on your wall?

Me: Seriously.

Shauna: You NEED to go to this concert. YOU! If I don't go, I will be bummed, but my heart won't be broken. I don't want your heart to be broken. I like your heart in one piece.

Me: Shauna = good friend. :)

Shauna: ;)

I come to the dinner table completely composed and rational. I promise myself that I will take three bites before I even mention Rory Calhoun. But even in my calm temporary silence, I wear my Rory Calhoun button on my shirt, the one I got at the mall, just to show her how serious I am.

I pull out my chair slowly and sit down next to Billy, who's already eating. Tonight, it's just my mom and Billy and me—my dad has a work dinner, and Cheryl's friends are taking her to a Burger King in another town where she's not banned—so we have grilled cheese. I don't even see a vegetable anywhere on the table, which is awesome.

We eat our grilled cheese in silence for a while, even Billy, his Darth Vader mask sitting in the chair next to him, and then my mom gives me a shy, knowing smile.

"I like your button," she says.

I shrug a little bit, like it's no big deal, but my eyes say, *Please?*

We each take another bite. One more bite, and I will carefully mention my life-changing request. But my mom beats me to the punch.

"Listen, Millie," she says. "I know that this is important to you. You clearly want this very much." I nod my head quickly with my hands over my mouth, both in wild anticipation of what this could mean for me and also to keep my mouth shut so I don't say something stupid and ruin it all.

"And," she continues, "I also have something that is very important to me."

What is she talking about? I'm very nervous as she continues.

"I think now that you're getting older, it's time you a make a larger contribution to this household," she says.

"What . . . you mean, like, get a job?"

"No, no, no . . ." She smiles. "I mean, just taking regular responsibility for something that helps us all out. Like maybe you could be in charge of cleaning the upstairs bathroom. Regularly. Like on a regular basis."

"That's it?" I say.

"Well . . . yes . . ." She seems surprised by my response. "But you'd have to do a good job. And, like I said, regularly. Not just once or anything."

What she doesn't know is that I would do way more than clean the upstairs bathroom *regularly* to see Rory Calhoun. I would clean all of our bathrooms plus all the neighbors' bathrooms and even all the bathrooms at school, including the boys' bathrooms, where I've heard they pee everywhere but inside the toilet. In other words, she totally underestimated me.

"But if I do a good job, *regularly* of course, you will buy Rory Calhoun tickets?"

"Yes," she says. "I will buy you Rory Calhoun tickets."

That's all I needed to hear.

chapter 21

@rorycalhoun
Good morning to all my amazing fans! At my piano. Working on a special song. The beginning of true love is the best inspiration.

@rorycalhoun
Song almost finished. Lyrics and melody done. Bringing in the best producers to give it some soul. New love always needs a little soul.

@rorycalhoun
Such a big day for me. I had some heartbreak a while ago, and this should make it better.

@rorycalhoun
I'm loving this song! I think it explains exactly how I feel right now. I hope you like it too.

@rorycalhoun
Almost done. Here's a hint: I'm so happy!

@rorycalhoun
One more take, and then it's time to go pick up the new love of my life!

Dear RC,

Is this about your "Worldwide Crush"? Did you find her?
Just when my mom told me she would get me tickets to
your concert? This is so dumb—did I really think that
you would find me and love me? No, I didn't.

So why am I so sad?

Love and . . .
Millie

@rorycalhoun
Done! I hope you feel like dancing, cuz that's what I was
doing when I heard the final track!

The post includes a video of Rory in studio—he listens,
he smiles. His hands cover his face, then he pumps a fist and
jumps up and starts dancing. Everyone in the studio claps,
and then they all dance too.

@rorycalhoun
Song available tomorrow morning! And you'll also get a
peek at my new love. Thanks everybody for being there
for me.

Dear RC,

I feel funny-different. If some girl from Sweden or
Brazil or Schenectady is your "Worldwide Crush," I want
to know what she's like. Does she like Yahtzee and wear
a hat? Is she funny? I wonder if she's nonchalant, or if
she worries about stuff. I really hope she's nice.

Love,
Or maybe sincerely,
Millie

@rorycalhoun
Here she is! Her name is Happy, and she is the new love of my life!

Dear RC,

It's a dog! His new love is a dog! He spent all day yesterday writing a song about how excited he was to go pick up his new puppy! I am both so relieved and so touched-and so confused! And so happy!

Love and doggies!
Millie

@rorycalhoun
Go to rorycalhoun.com to download a bonus track dedicated to Happy. She makes me so HAPPY!

Dear RC,

I can't stand it . . . Is it possible to love you even more? Listen up, all you teenage boys: loving puppies makes you very, very cute!

And it's a *bulldog!* Pringles would be so happy if she only understood, well, anything. But it makes me happy because I, too, know the love of a good bulldog, and it's like something very important that we share, something from your heart place-not something dumb like a favorite color.

Love, love, LOVE,
Millie

I go to his website immediately to listen to the song, and guess what it's called? "Happy"! And it really is the happiest song ever; it's like you can hear him smiling. Is that possible? I swear, I can hear him smiling.

This song is totally old-school, like one of Cheryl's old Monkees albums, with just a guitar and some handclaps and his happy, smiling voice. It took me just three listens to learn the handclaps, which is good because the next morning, on the bus, we all listen to "Happy" all the way to school, and we do the handclaps, all of us, perfectly, like we're in a commercial for teenage happiness or something.

It's so cool.

@rorycalhoun
Photo shoot today for me and my best girl. Look for a poster of Happy and me in the next issue of *TeenTalk Weekly*!

Dear RC,

Waiting for my poster to come in the mail! And just THREE more days until tickets go on sale!

Love,
Millie

chapter 22

I'm just starting to fall asleep when my phone pings. I grab it quickly so I don't get in trouble for texting after bedtime.

Shauna: I changed my mind. I can't go.
Me: Can't go where? RORY CALHOUN?!
Shauna: No! Language camp.
Me: Oh. Why? You were so excited?
Shauna: What if everyone there is super Filipino and already knows the names of all the stuff? What if they all have Filipino moms who make Filipino food every night? Or Filipino dads, I guess. Whatever! What if they all hang out without me because I don't know what anyone is talking about?
Me: You have to go. It might be awkward and weird at first. But then you'll learn all the words, and you'll feel better, and you'll come home with lots of pen pals. Wouldn't that be nice?
Shauna: You sound like a mom right now.
Me: I know. Go brush your teeth.
Shauna: I don't think we even need your mom to chaperone us at the Rory Calhoun concert. You're all the mom I need.

Me: TWO MORE DAYS UNTIL TICKETS GO ON SALE!

Shauna: RORY CALHOUN, WE'RE COMING FOR YOU! (♥ ♥ ♥!)

chapter 23

Shauna: I did it! I signed up! I hope you're right about the pen pal thing.

Me: Clap, clap, clap! YAY! I can't find the pencil emoji!

Shauna: Why do you need a pencil emoji?

Me: Writing letters to pen pals, dum-dum.

Shauna: Oh! In the olden days maybe. I'll prob just use my laptop.

Me: Then why is it a pen pal? That would be a laptop pal.

Shauna: Good point. And also, is your mom sitting by the phone with her credit card? ONE MORE DAY UNTIL TICKETS GO ON SALE!

Me: I don't know if I can take it. I've never been this excited for anything in my whole entire life. It's almost like my life begins tomorrow.

chapter 24

My mom has assured me that she knows how to buy tickets online. I leave her the website just in case, but she just laughs at me. "Go to school!" she says, and shoves me out the door.

At ten o'clock, I'm in language arts, and Ms. Hempel is explaining the importance of commas. I glance at the clock at 9:58 a.m. and get butterflies in my stomach. I watch the second hand go around once, twice, until the minute hand is pointing straight up at the twelve. Taking in a deep breath, I close my eyes and picture my mom sitting at her computer ordering tickets.

"Millie? Are you okay?"

I open my eyes and see that every head in the class is turned around and looking at me. Ms. Hempel asks again, "You okay, hon?"

I straighten up quickly and say, "Mm-hmm." Then I touch my temple and massage it like I might have a headache or something.

"You sure, sweetie?" she says.

"Yep." I nod my head and smile, then pick up my pencil to show that I'm ready to use commas.

After class, I go to my locker and check my phone. Nothing. I thought maybe my mom would text a little thumbs-up or something when she got tickets.

I check my phone between the next two classes, but still there's nothing. Finally, at lunch, I send her a text asking, "Tickets?" But I immediately get a "Message Send Failure" response. Schmidt! That explains why I haven't heard from her. Because my mom buys the cheapest cell service, I sometimes get no reception inside school on cloudy days, I swear. My mom says that's impossible—that cheapness and clouds have nothing to do with my reception—but I know that it's true. And because it's raining, we don't get to go outside for outdoor free-choice time, where I could actually use my phone. Double Schmidt!

So I do deep breathing for the rest of the day and think positive affirmations in order to keep myself from freaking out. The one on my mom's laptop says, "Breathe in calm, breathe out chaos," so I repeat that in my head when I start to feel anxious. I actually consider faking a stomachache so I can go to the nurse and call my mom. But instead, I stay in my seat and breathe in more calm and breathe out more chaos.

Finally, at the end of the day, the bell rings, and I race outside to the bus, where I can get some reception. I don't even wait for Shauna, walking and texting at the same time, hoping she can just catch up to me.

Me: Did you get them?

It takes several excruciating minutes for her answer, which is so typical. By the time I get a response, Shauna is sitting next to me on the bus. And this is what we see:

MOM: I will!

Oh my God. Shauna and I look at each other. Her eyes are wide with panic.

Me: What do you mean, 'I will'?
MOM: I just finished my last appointment.
Me: You didn't get them at 10:00 a.m.???????
MOM: I haven't been home. Emergency at work. On my way right now.

Triple Schmidt!

"No running!" The bus driver tries to slow us down, but we ignore him because this is a real emergency. We run toward our houses while Shauna reviews the plan so I know what to do.

"Go straight to your laptop so you can get a place in line!" she says breathlessly. "Then scream to see if your mom is home. If not, then call her so you can get her credit card number. I'll do the same, and one of us will get tickets! If we get too many tickets, we'll just sell them and make a huge profit! Don't waste time! Go! I'll call you!"

We split off, and I do as I'm told. I run in the house and go straight to my room. I hear Cheryl yell, "Shut the door!" but I don't stop.

I run up the stairs, peeling my backpack off my shoulders, dropping it on my way up. I can hear it tumble down the stairs behind me, but I don't care. When I get to my room, I lunge for the desk chair and yank it out so I can sit. The leg gets caught on the rug. Stupid chair! Gobsmackit! I sit down and click on the link I've had saved on the screen since the concert was announced—all in one motion.

The website asks me to wait "due to a high volume of traffic," and I get nervous about all the people getting tickets at that very moment when I'm in line *behind* them. I scream out, like we planned, "Mom! Cheryl!" I don't even know who's home. I yell, hoping I can get somebody's credit card in my hand quickly.

"No yelling in the house!" Cheryl yells this from downstairs somewhere. She yells way louder than I did.

The website is spinning. Open! Open! This is unbearable.

I hear a garage door open and then my mom's voice. "Hello, everyone!"

"Millie is upstairs yelling for you," Cheryl tells my mom. "I told her no yelling in the house."

"Thanks, Cheryl." My mom does not sound like she's in a hurry.

Finally, after what was probably thirty seconds but feels like thirty minutes, I'm in. "Mom!" Number of tickets, best available, press submit—yes! "Mom!"

Enter credit card number.

"Mom! Mom! I need your credit card number! Hurry!"

The phone rings. It's Shauna. I don't even say hello; I just start talking at her. "My mom just walked in. I'm on the site right now. And there's this clock thing on the screen, and it's counting backward, and it's making me nervous! I'll call you back!" I put my phone down and yell, "Moooooooooom!"

Billy comes running in with his Darth Vader mask on. I've scared him. "Why are you screaming?!"

"I need Mom! Now!"

"Is it a snake?"

"No! Snakes don't come in the house! Go get Mom for me, now! It's an emergency!" Darth Vader, bless his heart, runs away and does as he's told.

Almost immediately, my mom is standing in the door holding Billy's hand, with her purse still on her shoulder. "Millie! What is it?!"

"I need your credit card number!"

"What?!" She's gone from worried to mad in about one nanosecond. "I come running all the way up here because I think you're *dying*, and you tell me you want my credit card number?! Not funny, young lady. *Not* funny!"

"It's for the tickets, Mom! The tickets you said you would get, but you didn't! There are still some left, but I need to get them now!"

Suddenly, she understands and opens her purse, digging for her wallet. "Oh, I'm sorry, sweetie, I tried earlier but we had this woman come in who didn't know she was pregnant, and it turned into kind of an emergency situation, so I just thought I'd wait until I got home and . . ." She finds her wallet and pulls out the credit card.

Then the phone rings again. My mom grabs my phone before I do. "Hello?" She looks at me and whispers, "It's Shauna." Then she stands there with her credit card in her hand, trying to chitchat with Shauna. "Hi, sweetie! I haven't seen you since the block party!"

"*Mom!* The credit card! *Now!*"

"Oops. Hold on one sec," she says, confused. And instead of handing me the credit card, she hands me the phone.

I take the phone and hold it to my ear and hear Shauna say the words "sold out." But I don't care. I'm not giving up. My screen is still asking for my credit card. "I'll call you back," I say, and hang up without waiting for an answer.

"Mom! Credit card number! *Now!* Just read me the numbers! There's this clock thing counting backward . . . It says thirty-six seconds . . . Tickets are selling really fast . . . Oh my God! Thirty-three seconds!"

"Okay! Okay!" she says, panicking, and starts reading me numbers. "*Four!*"

I enter four. "Yes!"

"Seven!"

I enter seven. "Yes!"

"Nine!"

"Yes! Go faster!"

"Two, three, eight!"

"Yes!"

My brother's Darth Vader mask is looking right then left, right then left, following our manic conversation like he's watching a game of Ping-Pong. Until . . .

"Wait . . . what just happened?" The screen freezes. Then it reloads. "No! No, no, no, no, no, no!" Every time I say "no," I pound on the return key.

"What happened?" My mom leans over me to look at the screen. "Oh, honey . . . Oh no . . . I'm sorry. Oh my goodness, I'm so, so sorry."

"SOLD OUT" is in big orange letters.

My chest immediately fills with hate. I hate my mom. I hate her. I hate her. So. Much.

"Sweetheart . . . I don't know what to say. I didn't know it would go so fast."

My head drops to the keyboard, and I feel a surge of tears burning my lashes, fighting to get out. My mom reaches out to caress the back of my head . . . but I lift my forearm and block her.

"Okay . . . well . . . we can talk about this when you're ready, okay? I'm sorry, hon." She backs out of the room a little sheepishly. I can feel her turn around and look at me before she goes down the stairs.

Billy is still standing there. When she's gone, he lays his big Darth Vader head on my back and pats me gently. "Poor Millie."

And that's when I start to cry.

chapter 25

When I'm done crying, all I can do is get in my bed and close my eyes. I just want to go to sleep. Billy comes in my room and tells me it's time for dinner. I tell him I don't want dinner.

A few minutes later, my mom comes in. She tells me we're having lasagna, like I'm a dog and food makes me so happy that it erases everything that came before it. But I stay under my covers with my eyes closed and tell her I'm not hungry.

I can hear them downstairs eating. I hear the clatter of plates and silverware. I hear the low hum of voices. But I can't hear what they're saying.

Cheryl comes in later and sits on my bed. She pats my back and tells me she's sorry about Richard Calhoun. I think about correcting her, but I don't have the energy.

chapter 26

At the bus stop the next morning, we are a group divided. Half of us are glowing and squealing with excitement, and half of us are quiet and defeated. Shauna and I sit next to each other, but we say nothing. We are the defeated.

The school day will be painful; I will be sitting in social studies or Earth science with people who will live out the fantasy that was supposed to be mine. It's not easy living with the knowledge that your mom just messed up the rest of your life. She doesn't know about the "Worldwide Crush" part—she just thinks I'm missing a concert.

At home, I've begun to come out of my room, and every encounter with my mom involves a conversation like this: "I thought tickets *went on sale* at 10:00 a.m.; I thought it was just *starting* at 10:00 a.m. I didn't know I had to *buy* them at 10:00 a.m."

"Have you never bought tickets to a really big concert?" I scream. "You have to get them at 10:00 a.m. on the dot, or they're gone!"

"Honey, when was the last time I went to a 'really big concert'?" she says, using finger quotes. "Do you have any memory of me at all ever going to a 'really big concert'?" Finger quotes again. "The last time I went to a 'really big concert'"—finger quotes—"was when you were four, and I took you to see the Okee Dokee Brothers at the library. So, no, I did not know I had to get them at 10:00 a.m. on the dot." She's mad now. *She* messed up, and she's mad at *me*. It makes no sense.

So I just try to avoid her. I don't say much. I hang out in my room. When she asks me a question, I give a short answer and pretend I have to get something in another room. I'm trying not to be a complete brat, but it's hard. My mom is also trying not to be a complete brat; after we stop arguing about what "goes on sale at 10:00 a.m." means, she tries to be nice and chitchat with me, but she also gives me my space. And that makes me sad—she's allowing me to be mean to her because she knows she messed up everything. So I am both mad at my mom and so sad that I'm being so mean to her. This sucks.

Mostly, I stay in my room with Pringles. She gives me comfort, partially because I can think about Rory's new puppy, and partially because I chose her, and I love her, and she can look at me with those dumb dog eyes, and, I swear, it feels just like a hug.

Wipe your tears and look at me.
Right here in my arms is where you need to be.
They don't understand you, everyone can see.
But I do.
And I promise you, girl,
I will make it alright.
For you, I will make it alright.

—from "Make It Alright"
Music and lyrics by Rory Calhoun

chapter 27

Dear RC,

Today when I heard "Worldwide Crush" on the radio, I felt different. My chest felt like it was gripping something, squeezing. It might have been a sob. Will I not be able to listen to this song anymore? Or is it just indigestion?

Love and sadness,
Millie

After what seems like years of waiting, I see the new issue of *TeenTalk Weekly* at the grocery store with my mom, the one with Rory's photo shoot with Happy. My mom and I have reached a chilly détente in our relationship. That's a social studies vocab word that means "the easing of hostility or strained relations." Essentially, we are not yelling at each other anymore, but I just don't talk to her much.

I carefully slide the magazine out from its home between *Girls' Life* and *Weeknight Slow Cooker Recipes* and let it fall open to the glossy, folded poster inside. Have you ever felt your skin get prickly when something dramatic happens, like a rush of stars landing on your skin? Because that's what happens to me when I lay eyes on that poster of Rory cuddling his bulldog puppy. Holy Christmas.

This will be the first time I've said anything besides "yes," "no," or "I don't know" to my mom in forever. "Mom! Mom! I need this!" I say, holding the magazine to my chest.

She looks up—startled that I'm speaking to her—but gathers herself to look at the thing I'm clutching so desperately.

"Millie, you have a subscription to *TeenTalk*. Why would you buy it in the store?"

"Because it has a poster in it that I need!"

"Your copy won't come with the poster?"

"Well, yes, it will, but mine isn't here yet, and who knows how long it will take? This is here right now!"

"Sweetheart, that makes no sense. You want me to spend money for something that I've essentially already spent money for and will soon arrive in my mailbox?"

"Mom! Please! If you saw the poster, you would understand!"

"All right, let me see it." I open the magazine, and she looks at Rory and his faint freckles and his caring eyes with his arm cradling what looks like a little baby Pringles. "Oh my God, I'm such a sucker. Put it in the cart."

Thank you, Rory Calhoun, for being so cute. And thank you, Mom, for perhaps feeling a little bit guilty about ruining your daughter's life.

At home, I put the poster on my wall and sit down on my bed to stare at it and stare at it. I just keep staring at it. It seriously makes my heart hurt. And I wonder if he'll bring Happy out onstage with him during the concert. I would die, just die. It would probably be one of the cutest moments in music history.

Why, oh why, did life give me this stinking pile of dog poop bad luck? After I prayed to God and/or Jesus and everything? Is it because I never went to Sunday school? And is it too late for me now? Meaning God and/or Jesus will never listen to me about anything? Ever? My parents have *no idea* how many ways they've messed up my life.

Dear RC,

What about this . . . Could I win tickets in a contest? If there was a contest to find the person who knows the most about Rory Calhoun, I could definitely win. Ask me anything. Seriously! Anything!

The contest could even be televised. All the contestants would take their places behind their buzzers and face the studio audience. Every time the host asks a question, we buzz frantically—"What does Rory call his backup dancers? . . . What does Rory's shirt say on the cover of his first album? . . . Who taught Rory to play 'Let It Be,' his first song on the guitar?"—but all the other contestants answer incorrectly. I am always last. I always have the right answer.

"The Rory Pack . . . Bodega Bay Oyster Company . . . his mom."

"Wow, Millie is on fire!" the host would say.

Eventually, there are only two contestants left, me and a mean girl from a rich suburb.

"Ladies, this is your final question. Whoever answers this correctly will be our grand prize winner. What is Rory Calhoun's favorite soda?"

The mean, rich girl smirks at me and pushes her buzzer. "Dr Pepper!" she shouts.

"Ooooh, sorry, that is incorrect. Let's see if our other contestant knows the answer. Millie, what is Rory Calhoun's favorite soda?"

I look nonchalantly at the mean, rich girl, who is pouting now, and I slowly and calmly say, "Pibb. It's Pibb."

"Congratulations, Millie Jackson! You've won front-row tickets to the Rory Calhoun concert in Hollywood, California! You will fly first-class and stay at the same hotel where Rory is staying! The next day, you and Rory will share a one-of-a-kind day, including horseback riding on the beach and sharing an ice cream cone!"

Then I would go straight to the airport and get picked up by a limousine in Hollywood. At the concert, I would sit in the front row, and of course, Rory would choose me as his "Worldwide Crush" girl. I wouldn't cry; I would stick to the plan in which I just smile and hold his hand to my heart. And when he hugs me at the end of the song, he would whisper in my ear, "Meet me backstage. Please. I need to see you again."

So I would watch the rest of the concert from the wings, and at the end, he would come running off and strip off his shirt because he's so sweaty. And he would grab a towel and dab at his face and his smooth chest, and some guy would give him a bottle of water and say, "Great show, Rory!" And Rory would shake his hand and say, "Thanks, man. No, really, thank you. That means a lot."

He doesn't see me, but he seems to be looking around. "Is she still here?" he would ask, still dabbing at his smooth chest with the towel. Someone points to me waiting, and he would shyly come over and say, "Hi, I'm

Rory Calhoun." Which is so funny because *of course* I know that!

And that's when I would find out that the game show was created by Rory himself so he could find a special someone who truly understands him. "You know me better than anyone. That's what I need. I need you." And then he would press his cheek against mine. I would wrap my arms around his waist. And we would stand there like that, still, while everyone watches. They've never seen Rory like this before. One person starts to clap slowly. Then someone else joins in. And pretty soon, everyone is clapping because Rory has finally found his "Worldwide Crush."

And then we get married and get a dog. Her name is Funyuns.

Love and stuff,
Millie

And just like that, MomTalk Radio 107.1 is having a contest! If you can dream it, you can be it! Or whatever that saying is! It's not a quiz show, but I could still win. It's called Best Mom of All Time, and they're inviting moms to call in and make their daughters' dreams come true! All you have to do is listen for them to play "Worldwide Crush" and be the 107th caller—because you can't be the 107.1th caller. The winner gets two tickets to the Rory Calhoun concert in Minneapolis; plus, you get picked up in a limousine! At first, I planned to ask my mom to listen and call in, but she has proved to be incompetent and unreliable. So I will do it myself. I'm sure I can dial faster than most moms anyway. I will just try to sound grown-up and tell them my name is

Ms. Millicent Jackson. My daughter's name will be Anastasia or Felicity. It's on Saturday, so I can devote every minute of my day to this task. How many moms are really going to do that? They will have to run errands or pay bills or something. I think my chances are very good!

Dear RC,

I've been listening to MomTalk Radio all day. I've learned about the first signs of menopause, asking for a raise at work, how to hide vegetables in brownies, and how to keep the spark alive in your marriage (this was gross-some stuff I would like to unhear). But so far they have not played "Worldwide Crush." And the day is almost over. Next up is an interview with a lady who has a special gift for stain removal, and she will share her secrets with us. This is exhausting.

Love,
Millie

Dear RC,

They've played every Rory Calhoun song but "Worldwide Crush." I started to wonder if I had misunderstood the directions, so when I heard the intro to "Sunshine Girl," I quickly dialed 612-MOM-TALK. I asked if I won, and the lady sounded irritated and said, "It's not 'Worldwide Crush'! You have to call during 'Worldwide Crush'!" And then she hung up on me. So now at least I am clear about the directions.

Not giving up,
Millie

Dear RC,

After seven hours and thirty-three minutes of listening to MomTalk, they finally played "Worldwide Crush." I dialed the number 117 times in a row—beep, beep, beep, busy signal, hang up, beep, beep, beep, busy signal, hang up. I did that 117 times. I did it until the song ended and I heard the voice on the radio say, "We have a winner!" It was not me. It was some lady from Fargo, North Dakota. I don't know why a lady from so far away is listening to this station. Is the limo going to go all the way to North Dakota to pick them up for the concert? I think she should be disqualified.

Love in sadness,
Millie

chapter 28

Late last night, I hear my mom talking to Cheryl after the news. Cheryl is saying motherly things and trying to make my mom feel better. I'm not sure, but I think my mom is crying a little bit.

I sit at the top of the stairs, hidden from view, and I hear Cheryl say, "Carrie, it's not you, I promise. The Rudy Calhoun thing was very unfortunate, but—"

"It's Rory," my mom sniffs.

"Yes, whatever, but she's almost a teenager, and her hormones are starting to surge, and she doesn't know what to do with them. Every tragedy is felt so deeply—*so* deeply. But it's not you, sweetheart. She'll bust out of this soon and come back to us. I promise."

I tiptoe back into my room and climb into bed with my clothes on. Then I get up again and scoop Pringles up off my rug, which is not easy because she is so fat, and I nestle her on my bed so she can be sad with me.

The next morning, my alarm doesn't go off. I accidentally set my alarm for 7:30 p.m. instead of 7:30 a.m. Gob! So I oversleep and miss the bus, and my mom has to drive me to school.

When we arrive, she gets out of the car with me, which is totally unnecessary, and she opens the hatchback and hands me my backpack, which I totally could've gotten by myself. "Here you go, girlfriend," she says, like she's some kind of cool hipster parent.

I take my backpack from her and say, "Mom, could you please not call me 'girlfriend'?"

"What? Why not?" She looks a little hurt.

"Because you're my mom."

"Yeah, but I'm a cool mom." She winks at me.

"What if I don't want a cool mom? What if I just want a mom who acts like a mom?"

"Oh . . . I get it," she says. "Sorry, sweetie."

"Not 'sweetie' either," I say.

Her shoulders fall, and she hangs her head briefly. "I'm so confused," she says. "What exactly do you want then, Millie?"

After the conversation I overheard last night, I'm not sure what to say. "I just want you to act like a mom. But one who doesn't love me too much." It's so hard to explain that to parents—too much love is embarrassing.

Her hands are on her hips, and she shakes her head. "Man, that is tough. But I'll try. I'll try not to love you so much." She smiles just a little bit. "Maybe I can come up with some mom-ish but unloving word to call you. Like 'hey you.' Or 'girl.' How's that? I'll call you 'girl.'"

"Very funny, Mom," I say, and turn to walk toward the school doors. And she starts to come with me. "You have to stop here," I say. "You can't walk me in anymore, or people will think I need my Mommy to help me find my locker or something."

"Yes—okay," she says, sighing. "It's all part of today's theme, isn't it? Well . . . then . . . Godspeed, girl. Be on your way—independently. Have a very plain day. I have neutral feelings for you." Here she holds out her hand like she wants to shake hands. I roll my eyes instead. But it's hard not to laugh.

And as I walk away, I think I hear her say, very quietly, "Love you, Millie."

chapter 29

As concert day gets closer, the cloud over my head feels heavier. I thought it would get easier as time went on, but it actually gets worse. Each day, the lucky ticket holders get more and more excited. And their RC crushes get more and more dramatic. The lunchroom is like a Rory Calhoun lovefest to which I am not invited.

I feel a kind of sadness that makes you look at the ground all the time. I seriously think it would've been easier if my mom had never said yes, if she had just said I couldn't go in the first place. Instead, it feels like I was given this most amazing, life-changing gift—and then somebody broke it. And I see that life-changing gift shattered in pieces on the floor while the person who broke it just walks away, like it doesn't even matter.

My mom broke my gift. She knows it. And she feels bad. But she also thinks my "hormones" are making me "overly dramatic" about it. And her solution to this hormone problem is a mother-daughter retreat. An *all-day* mother-daughter retreat. And would you like to know the name of this all-day mother-daughter retreat? Get ready . . . Here it is: You, Me, & Puberty: Talking about Our Changing Bodies!

Oh God, please no . . .

I beg her. I plead. I tell her I love her and that I'll never not love her again. But she thinks it will be fun. Fun *how*?!

～

We pull up in front of a church with a scrolling LED sign out front that reads: FAMILY JAM! JESUS ROCKS THE HOUSE WEDNESDAY NIGHTS AT 6:30! I picture a room full of moms and dads dancing awkwardly, thinking this will finally convince their kids that Jesus really does rock the house. I reluctantly heave myself out of the car, and my mom and I follow the signs that say, YOU, ME, & PUBERTY! IN THE FELLOWSHIP HALL! Even the signs embarrass me—what if someone sees me reading signs about puberty? Eventually, they lead us down the stairs to a dark conference room in the basement with an accordion-style room divider and rust-colored carpeting, stained. Probably made by spilled coffee, because this looks like the place people go after funerals to drink coffee and discuss the deceased.

We're greeted by a beige-looking woman, named Kate, with dry skin, and she tells us many, many times how excited she is that we are joining them today(!). Then she makes us sign a whole bunch of forms claiming, I assume, that they can't be held responsible if we are emotionally scarred in any way by today's presentation.

She says once again that she is super excited that we've joined them today, and she asks us to take a seat in the circle of kindergarten-sized chairs.

Once we're seated, a man comes over to us—a *man*!— and he also tells us how excited he is that we've decided to join them today. And I'm like, oh God, no—how is a man going to teach me about my changing body? He speaks with a heavy accent, like he's from Russia or France or something.

His name is Peter, I think. It could also be some French name that I don't know.

The other girls are coming in with their moms, and they are also greeted by Kate and Peter(?). I'm sure they're super excited that they have joined us today—and these girls all look significantly younger than me, like nine-year-olds or something. What do nine-year-olds care about puberty? They are smiling and happy to be here, like they have no idea how embarrassing this is, and their changing bodies look relatively unchanged. Even with my practically empty sports bra, I feel like a giant who flunked You, Me, & Puberty the first time and now I'm back for another try.

Peter picks up a tom-tom and lightly drums while people mill around and find their seats. He closes his eyes and sways just a little bit. I worry that he's going to make us all play the tom-tom while we talk about our changing bodies. I start to sweat.

After a few minutes, Peter gets up and strolls around the circle while he drums, pausing in front of each mother-daughter pair with his eyes closed, as if he's casting a puberty spell on them or something. Some people look up and smile, like they're watching a mariachi band at a Mexican restaurant—and others pretend to be doing other things, like looking for items in their purses or checking for split ends. When he gets to us, I work to get something out of my eye. My mom half smiles at him and half looks for something in her purse, as if she can't decide if she's excited or uncomfortable.

When Peter is done casting his puberty spells, he takes a seat next to Kate and opens a binder to begin the program.

"Good morning, everyone." His accent is both romantic and confusing. "We are so excited that you have joined us today so that we can help you on your journey to womanhood. I am privileged to be your guide. I have a young daughter named Ariel"—he says it like "Arr-ee-el"—"who is thirteen years old. And her puberty has been a wonder to me. There is so much I learn by discussing her changes with her."

Oh my God, poor Arr-ee-el! What if my dad was in awe of my puberty?! I think I would rather ride the bus in my underwear.

"And now I would like Kate to welcome you all with a special ceremony. Kate, would you be so kind as to continue, please?"

Kate begins. "Let's honor our presence here today by thanking Mother Earth and each other."

Here she picks up some pieces of garbage on a low table in front of her. It looks like some grass clippings, a broken stick, and some schmutz from the sidewalk.

"I'd like you to hold these pieces of Mother Earth in your hand and say, 'Thank you, Mother Earth.' Then pass the pieces of Mother Earth to your neighbor, who will continue the circle of gratitude."

What do grass clippings have to do with my puberty? When it's my turn, I look at the garbage in my hand as if I'm really thanking it hard, just so I don't have to look anyone in the eye.

Our first activity of the day is making a 3D model of the female reproductive system using yarn, straws, red napkins, masking tape, and plastic Easter eggs. Peter is wandering around, admiring our work and making comments, which all contain body-part words that I'd rather not say out loud. He says, "I can really see the vaginal canal!" Except with his accent it sounds like "vah-*zhee*-nal ca-*nol*." And I'm worried that these younger girls, who have never heard the words "vaginal canal," are going to go back to school tomorrow and start talking about their "vah-*zhee*-nal ca-*nols*."

The vah-zhee-nal ca-nol exercise is followed by the writing of mother-daughter haikus; a sing-along of "The Sperm and the Egg" sung to the tune of "The Wheels on the Bus"—I am completely serious about this; and Body Image Bingo, in which the winner has to say something positive about their body. All I can think of is that my arms aren't as hairy as some people's. And finally, Kate jumps up dramatically and sings, "Now it's time for the most popular part of our day: Mother-Daughter Ball! Yaaaaaaaaaay!" She waves her hands around all crazy, like this simple action will convince us that this will be fun.

My mom and me, we're not stupid. We know what this is. This is dodgeball. I'm more than a little worried right now because my mom and I are not exactly roughhousing types. We're more into clever wordplay than dodgeball. My mom actually tells stories of the things she used to do as a kid to get out of dodgeball, like yelling, "Rats!" and walking over to the bench like she's out, when the ball never even touched her. The walk to the gym feels like a death march—why does this church have a gym? But as we walk through the double doors, my mom dips her face close to mine and whispers, "Stay close, and follow my lead." Then she grabs the back of my shirt and starts taking slow, careful steps backward, away from the crowd of moms and daughters.

I can't believe this—my mom is helping me ditch class. She sneaks out so expertly that I wonder if she's done this before.

As we walk backward, I whisper out of the side of my mouth, "Are we skipping?"

"Shh," she says.

Once out the door, we sit down on the floor, just out of sight, and watch through a narrow window as grown women get smacked in the head with playground balls. Each time we hear the ball make contact, we silently fist-bump.

When I see my mom peeking through the glass, trying not to be seen, she doesn't look like a mom at all. Right there in that moment, she is no different from me—just a kid trying to get out of stupid dodgeball because dodgeball is so dumb. A mom would have pretended to be all excited and tried to change my mind about dodgeball. A mom would have said, "Just try it! You'll see how fun it is!" even though she doesn't believe it.

As uncomfortable as this day has been, I feel just then like I should tell my mom that I don't hate her; everyone here seems so worried about their children loving them. But not loving our moms is not super realistic—don't they know that?—it's just that we don't climb up into their laps and kiss them on the lips anymore. And maybe that's sad for them.

When the last person gets smacked in the head, the game is finally over. My mom and I stand up and slyly fall in with the other moms and daughters as they make their way back to the fellowship hall, and we smile knowingly at each other. She starts to put her arm around my shoulders but then stops.

"Don't worry," she whispers in my ear. "I won't hug you in front of all these people. *But I want to!*"

That could be the kindest thing my mom has ever said to me.

And instead of hugging, we just nudge each other in the ribs about a thousand times.

Kate begins as soon as we all find our chairs. "Welcome back, everybody. We have just one more activity before we end the day with another special ceremony. The Question Box gives you the opportunity to ask questions anonymously—things about your body, relationships, reproduction, anything. This is a safe place. And, as I'm sure you've all figured out already, we don't embarrass easily. This is for moms too. Because we all have questions about things." She smiles and begins passing out turquoise sticky notes and tiny golf pencils.

I take my pieces of paper and find a private spot in the room while everyone scratches away with their pencils. I see my mom chew on her pencil and start writing. What is she writing? Is it possible that she doesn't know something?

I only have one question: Is it true that some ladies wax the hair off of their you-know-whats? If yes, why? This is something I heard on the bus.

The answer is yes—ouch, why?!—and has something to do with how the media portrays women. And swimsuits. And then there is also some stuff about sex, but it's gross so I try to look like I'm not listening. When I accidentally make eye contact with my mom, she mimes sticking her finger down her throat and then mouths the words "Oh my God, please shut up!" I try to remain disinterested, but it's hard not to laugh at her.

Some of the other questions include: Is it bad to tickle yourself in the armpit? How do you become a lesbian? What does "horny" mean? And finally—should I be worried about my daughter's obsession with a pop music star?

Immediately, my face burns like fire. I imagine everyone turning around to look at me. And now, in this horrible moment, I understand why we're here—it's not my hormones, it's that she thinks I'm a freak.

I don't even look at my mom. I'm so embarrassed, I just move toward the door, trying not to run and also trying not to cry until I make it outside this room. My mom gets up too and follows me just as quickly, so I walk faster. When we reach the hallway, she calls out, "Mille!" in this whispering, yelling kind of way.

"Millie!" she whisper-yells again. "Stop it! Where are you going? You don't even know where you are!"

This time I twirl around. "How could you?!" I say, mid-sob. I've seen myself cry before, so I know my face is red and blotchy.

"I didn't!"

"Am I really that embarrassing to you?!" I turn and run up the stairs, not waiting for an answer, but before I get too far, she grabs my wrist and pulls me back.

"I said I didn't!" She spins me around. "I didn't write that question!"

I blink twice. "You didn't?" It never for a minute occurred to me that it could've been someone else's mom.

"No! I don't even think you're obsessed. But even if you were, I wouldn't care."

"Well," I say, confused, wiping my eyes. "Who did it then?"

"Does it matter?" she says. "It's not about you."

"So that means that it's someone else in there?"

She grabs me by the shoulders. "Yes! Probably all of them. What, you think you're the first person to ever feel like this? My God, Millie, I still have my Leonardo DiCaprio poster in the attic. I know that sounds weird, and please don't tell your father, but, honey"—she pulls me closer—"if there's anything we've learned today, it's that this is a very difficult time for girls your age and—"

I push her away and interrupt. "I'm not sad because of puberty! God, Mom!" I bring my hands to my temples in disbelief. "I'm sad because my heart is broken! There was something I wanted so badly that could've changed my whole life, and it was taken away from me! It has nothing to do with hormones or growing up or our relationship or anything! Just let me be sad!"

"Oh . . . okay," she says quietly. "I'll let you be sad. I just wish I could help." Then she looks down at the floor and says, "And I'm really sorry . . . like so, so sorry . . . that I couldn't get those tickets for you. And I don't know if I'll ever get over it." She looks almost as sad as I do.

I keep my head down, but I lean into her just a bit. And she carefully puts her arm around my shoulders—and I let her.

We walk back in just as we hear a mom ask a follow-up question. "Okay, so it's not unhealthy, but how do we help them see that this isn't real?"

Another mom says, "Yeah. And shouldn't we be teaching them to be independent instead of boy crazy?"

And Peter says in his lovely, romantic, confusing accent, "Boy crazy, girl crazy . . . It is *natural* to be attracted to people. It does not mean you're not independent. And also, why isn't this real? These feelings are very real, that is for sure. And for people this age, it's the most real relationship they've ever had. To invalidate it by saying it isn't real would be like telling your daughter that her feelings are not valuable, that her feelings are wrong. Do you really want your daughter to be ashamed of her feelings?"

The moms nod their heads. The daughters are checking for split ends.

"Mothers," Peter says, "crushes on celebrities are real, and they are intense, and they serve a purpose: they are an important step in learning how to be in love. It allows them to see who they are in a relationship. Stand back, ladies, and let them love these people until they are ready for something else."

My mom's arm tightens around me a little bit, and she gives me a few quick squeezes, like a secret hug, and we take our seats.

Looking satisfied, Kate gets up and walks over to a table by the door. "We would like to end our program with a parting gift. On this table is a grouping of rocks. On each of those rocks is a word. Mothers, on your way out, listen to those rocks; which one speaks to you the loudest?" Kate pauses to pick up a rock and caress it with her fingers.

"When you get home, you can give this rock to your daughter as a reminder of your time here today. Everyone's rock will have a different word because each of you will take home something different from today's experience."

And finally, thankfully, the program is over. I feel like running out the door, but the moms linger at the rock table, slowing down our exit. I grab the car keys from my mom, and I push through the crowd, making a dash for the car, a place I know will be free of humiliation. By the time my mom emerges from the church, I'm already in the car, my seat belt buckled and the radio on. I see her left hand curled around her rock as she approaches the car. She swiftly opens the door, sits down, and swings around to put her purse in the back seat. And then she turns toward me.

"What?" I say.

She turns off the radio and turns toward me again. And she opens her hand to reveal a teardrop-shaped stone.

She looks at the rock as she speaks. "I chose this one, not because of the word it had but because it was dark and smooth, and I wanted to hold it in my hand. Then I turned it over . . . and it said "Love." And I thought, well, that's appropriate. Because . . ."

And she stops.

"Because . . ." She chokes up a little bit. "There is . . ."

She starts strong but ends up whispering the word "nothing" so quietly that I can barely hear her. Her chin starts to wiggle, and she can't say any more. My mom takes my hand, puts the dark stone in the center, and closes my hand around it.

Then she wipes her eyes, turns the key in the ignition, and we drive away.

And I sit there holding her love in my hand.

chapter 30

That night, I feel like I can be honest with my mom, at least a little bit. My room is covered with whale collages and whale acrostics, and I've been dropping hints forever, but I don't feel like anyone is listening to me. Even when I came right out and asked her if we could go to California, she answered with a "you can do anything if you just work hard" speech. Nobody is listening to me. And that's exactly what I tell her.

She stops picking up laundry and turns to face me. "What do you mean, I'm not listening to you? I just spent the whole day listening to you."

"I'm talking about California, Mom. I just really, really want to go. And not like Disneyland or Hollywood or anything—I want to go to Bodega Bay. But every time I bring it up, people just make jokes or ignore me."

"Hmm . . ." She says it like she's remembering something. "The whales."

"Yeah, the whales." I say this a little quietly because it's starting to feel more like lying. But I'm also starting to like whales for real, a little more with each collage I make, so maybe by the time we got there, it wouldn't be a lie.

"Really, Mom. Seriously. We could do it for our next break! I could even do all the planning; you wouldn't have to do a thing! Please, Mom, can we go to Bodega Bay?" I look at her hard, like I'm waiting for an answer.

"Well, sure, I think someday that could be really great." She walks over to my bed and reaches for the covers to tuck me in. "Good night, sweetie." Then she kisses my forehead and walks away. She does not sound like she means this the way I want her to mean it.

But I'm not done, and I stop her before she goes out the door. "No, I mean it," I say. "Like, soon. We don't ever go anywhere except the water park hotel."

She turns around and looks tired standing there with her armful of laundry. "Honey, do you know how expensive airfare is for four people? It's, like, thousands of dollars." She pauses. "But you're right . . . the water park hotel is getting a little old, isn't it?"

"It's not even going anywhere. And it smells. I want to go someplace real, like a place that's different from here, you know?"

"What about Arizona? You love going to Great-Grandma Phyllis's condo in Arizona!"

She just *thinks* I love going to Phyllis's condo in Arizona, even though I've never said any such thing. That's what parents do—if you don't complain, they assume you love something.

"Mom, we *only* go to Arizona. Ever. Don't you want to try someplace new?"

She sighs. "Ahh . . . jeez, Millie, I don't know. I guess." She shifts the laundry around a little while she thinks. "Maybe we can drive to Jellystone Park for your next break? You kids always beg to go there every time we drive by." She comes back over and tucks me in with one hand. "Well, we can talk about it tomorrow. Night night, honey." She kisses me again and turns out the light as she leaves the room.

I haven't asked to go to Jellystone Park for years. I don't even really know what Jellystone Park is. But there's a big sign on the way to the Wisconsin Dells that has cartoon characters on it, and it says, FOOD AND FUN FOR EVERYONE! so of course we beg to go there. Food and fun sounds awesome when you've been in the car for three hours. The cartoon characters are not even from a cartoon that's still on TV.

This feels like another strikeout. But I'm not giving up.

If I save all my allowance and all my birthday money and all my babysitting money, maybe I'll have enough to go to California . . . when I'm eighty.

chapter 31

Dear RC,

The concert is tomorrow. I think I feel a tickle in my throat, like I'm getting sick. I don't think it's a good idea for me to go to school tomorrow. No one is listening in any of my classes anyway. They just smile and hyperventilate all day long. It's worse than the day before Christmas break—way worse.

I don't hyperventilate—I hypo-ventilate. Wouldn't that be the opposite of hyperventilate? I sit at my desk and look out the window, pretending I'm not there. And when Dr. Marion says, "I bet a lot of you will be going to the Rory Calhoun concert tomorrow, right?" I hide my sad truth. People nod and smile and look at each other like, *Omigod, I can't wait!* And I do a nodding thing too. I do it, even though it's a lie. I feel embarrassed. And sad. So very sad. So I nod.

Heavyheartedly,
Millie

chapter 32

I'm lying in my bed with a feeling of dread pinning me to the sheets.

I don't think I can get up.

I roll over and keep my eyes closed. Keeping them closed feels good. The longer I keep them closed, the longer I can pretend that this day isn't happening. Today is the day I'm not going to the Rory Calhoun concert. Thousands and thousands of people—many of them in the classes that I will sit in today—are going to lay eyes upon the only person I've ever loved. Most people will just see him from afar and be overjoyed to be in his actual in-the-flesh presence. But some will watch him write his name on scraps of paper, and some will talk to him as he walks by, and some will touch his hand as he reaches down from the stage for a group high five. And one lucky person—probably a girl because he said he's looking for a girl—will be chosen to come on stage. She will lock eyes with him, for a moment he will look at her and only her, and he will sing her a song that, on that day, is meant for her. And she will cry, because they all cry. She will cry because his words, his song, will go straight into her heart. And maybe, just maybe—super slim chance, but still—just maybe . . . he will fall in love with her.

I stay under the covers with my head buried under my pillow so I can't see my closet doors taunting me with the many faces of Rory Calhoun, knowing that his actual face, at this very moment, is just minutes away from me, somewhere in Minneapolis. His bed is just minutes away from my bed. But it doesn't matter.

Because I can't see him.

And I'll probably never see him.

The thought of going to school is terrifying. What am I going to do when The Blondes see each other and start squealing about what they're going to wear tonight? Apparently, Iris Moriarty's mom spent wads of cash for seats in the sixth row so Iris would have a shot at being the "Worldwide Crush" girl. For the past month, whenever The Blondes see each other in the halls, they wink and say, "Sixth row!"

What kind of mom does that? What mom spends money like that, in hopes of marrying off her daughter at the ripe old age of, oh I don't know, *just barely puberty*? Maybe they should take all those wads of cash and feed some starving children or something—just an idea. Freak.

I get out of bed and walk into my mom and dad's room. My mom is sleeping on her back with her forearm slung across her eyes, shutting out the day that is to come.

"Mom . . . Mom."

"Hmm . . ."

"I don't feel well. I think I should stay home."

She doesn't move.

"Mom . . . I don't feel well. My throat kinda hurts."

With her eyes still covered by her forearm, she mumbles her standard response to this request: "Do you have a test today?"

I don't know why she always says this. She must've read it in a parenting book about problem children or something, which I am not.

"No. I don't care about tests. I just don't feel well. My throat is a little scratchy."

"Hmm. Okay. I'll drive you to school. If you still don't feel well at lunch, go to the nurse, and I'll come get you." Her forearm doesn't move that whole time. It's like her speech is automatically generated while she sleeps. Someday she's going to send me to school with a broken leg or something, with instructions to go to the nurse if it doesn't get better by lunch.

Forget it. It was a lame attempt.

The most difficult part of the day comes in social studies. Karly Sanders sits next to me; we are social studies friends. I never see her any other time, but we whisper and pass notes when we are in here, because she likes Rory Calhoun too.

Just before the bell rings, she comes running over to me and says, "Millie! You got tickets!"

"What?" I say weakly, confused. I don't know what she's talking about, but I want to reach out and grab on to her words.

"Yeah! Are you going tonight?"

For a minute, my heart pounds—hard. My face gets hot. Could this be right? Like maybe I won a contest, and they just announced it on the radio, and everyone knows but me?

"No, Karly, that was Millie Sampson, not Millie Jackson." Theo, who sits at the table next to me, offers this without looking up from his phone that he's hiding under his desk. "It was, like, five hundred bucks or something stupid."

Oh—the other Millie, not me.

This is an unfortunate mix-up on this difficult day, as I actually hoped for a second that her words were true. And my face must show my disappointment, because Scott Fenwick, the kid who sits next to Theo, kicks his foot and says, "Shut up, man! God, you're so stupid."

Theo looks up from his phone and goes, "What?" but Scott rolls his eyes and shakes his head. It's embarrassing because my confusion and anguish must be so obvious.

"Oh . . . rats," Karly says, looking at me, also embarrassed. "Well . . . um," she continues, looking concerned, "did you finish your worksheet for today?"

I say yeah, but it comes out like a whisper because my throat is tight with disappointment. I actually believed for a millisecond that she could be right. Karly knows she rattled me; she keeps looking at me, a little worried, and she tries to say stuff that is totally unrelated, trying to change the subject.

"My brother got a tooth knocked out last night at hockey. It was gross. Blood all over the ice. Blech . . ."

During class, she passes me a note. I open it, and it says, "Guess what? (open flap)." I open the flap and it says, "Chicken butt!"

I look at her and roll my eyes. But then I laugh quietly, so Dr. Marion can't hear me, because it's so nice of her to try and make me feel better.

Then a note comes from the other direction, across the aisle. When Dr. Marion turns toward the board, Theo reaches out and swiftly deposits a neatly folded triangle in front of me. It says, "MILLIE" in all caps.

I unfold the triangle quietly and read it. "Sorry about the concert. I know you really wanted to go. That sux. ☹ Scott."

I look to my right and see Scott leaning back in his chair, chewing on his pencil while he listens to Dr. Marion talk about the civil rights movement.

He doesn't look at me. And I don't know if that means he's already moved on from this note or that he's embarrassed to look at me—like I'm embarrassed to look at him. I've never gotten a note from a boy, and I feel a little self-conscious that he knows me like this—the girl who likes Rory Calhoun. But I also feel like, if he weren't a boy, I would totally give him a hug right now.

At my locker after class, I can see that the face of my phone is glowing through the fabric of my backpack. I open the flap, pull it out, and see that there's a text from my mom:

MOM: I'm going to pick you up after school, K? Leaving here in five min.

It was sent just one minute ago. So I respond, quickly, seizing this moment of good reception.

Me: Okay. Why?

And she responds right away.

MOM: I have some news I want to tell you in person.

I get a nervous feeling in my stomach, like something bad has happened. Why would she pick me up when there's a perfectly good bus to ride? This is what she tells me when I ask for a ride.

Me: Is everything okay?
MOM: Yes, everything is fine. I just really want to deliver this news in person.
Me: Is Pringles okay?
MOM: Yes, Pringles is fine. Don't worry. It's all good.
Me: Okay. See u.

I'm still nervous, but I keep telling myself it's okay. She said everything is fine. She said everything is fine. She said everything is fine. But what the Frank could it *be*? Gob!

Shauna is waiting for me by the tall tree.

"My mom is picking me up! She said she has news that she has to give to me in person! I have no idea what it is! I'm a little bit nervous! I have no idea what it is! I guess I already said that!"

"Oh my God! Do you know what it is?"

"I said, I have no idea what it is!"

"Millie, are you moving?!"

"Holy Schmidt! I don't know! Oh my God, I don't want to move!"

"I don't want you to move! What would I do without you? Millie!"

"Stop it . . . Maybe it's just a trip to Disney World."

"Yes, it's probably Disney World."

I see my mom pull up behind the buses, and I give Shauna a worried look. "Call me," she says. "As *soon* as you can! ASAP! Promise!"

"Yes," I say. "Okay. I promise." I say it, but I'm not sure I can follow through if it's bad news. But my mom said it's all good. I really, really, really have to work hard to not be so nervous.

I walk over to the car, and I see my mom's eyes on me the whole time. She is smiling. Not a toothy grin like you do in pictures but a laser-focused, all-knowing "I'm gonna rock your world" happy face.

I run the last few steps, open the door, and sit down. "What?!" I say.

"Millie, I have some good news."

"Okay?"

"My coworker's daughter got caught smoking weed in their garden shed."

Huh? "I don't get it," I say.

"And she's grounded." She's still smiling.

"Is this a drug talk? Because I don't do drugs. I've never even seen drugs."

"No, Millie. This girl is grounded. And she's not allowed to use her tickets—" My mom's voice catches in her throat, like she's trying not to cry.

Oh my God.

"To the Rory Calhoun concert tonight."

I do not want to assume. I do not want to jump to conclusions, for fear of being disappointed.

I say nothing.

I look at her hard and wait for her to speak.

"Millie . . . she gave me her tickets."

And she really is crying—a little bit laughing and a little bit crying. And even though we are still sitting in front of school, and everyone can see me, I plunge my face into her neck and wrap my arms around her and squeeze. I squeeze like I haven't squeezed in years.

Me: Shauna!!! OMG!!!!!! My mom's coworker's daughter got caught smoking weed in her garden shed, and she got grounded, and she's not allowed to go the concert tonight, so SHE GAVE MY MOM HER TICKETS! My mom is taking me to see Rory Calhoun tonight!!!
Shauna: Whaaaaaat????????
Shauna: MILLIEEEEEE!!!!!!!!!!
Shauna: I'm dead.
Me: I KNOW!!!!!!!!!!!!!!
Shauna: MILLIEEEEEE!!!!!!!!
Me: I KNOW!!!!!!!!!!!!!!
Shauna: Are you Frankin' kidding me????????
Me: NOOOOOOOO!!!!!!!!!!!

Shauna: Holy hound dog. You deserve it. ☺

Me: Thank you. ☺ ☺ I wish you could go with me. ☹

Shauna: Me too. ☹☹

Me: Are you sad?

Shauna: Yes. But it's okay. You're his number one fan. I'm like his number thirty-seven fan.

Me: Do you want me to get you a T-shirt?

Shauna: Yes! And can you take video of "Rock Your Body, Girl"?

Me: Of course!

Shauna: And send it to me right afterward.

Me: Okay.

Shauna: Like RIGHT afterward. While you're still at the concert.

Me: For sure.

Shauna: Cool. Have a good time, friend. Luv u.

Me: ☺

chapter 33

We park the car in the big downtown parking ramp and follow the parade of people heading toward the Pop Tasty Bagel Bite Center. I've been downtown plenty of times, but I've never seen this many people before. It feels like every person that exists on the planet is walking in the same direction, and I can feel the excitement of every single one of them. I've wished for this for so long, and I dreamed about it in a way that made it feel impossible, like it could only happen in a movie. And now it's really happening.

At the corner, I see the crowd milling around in front. It's almost all girls. I know there have to be boys with crushes too, but I don't see any. Some girls are crying. Actually, many girls are crying. This makes me feel extremely mature and healthy, as if my crush on Rory Calhoun is not as wacky and obsessive as theirs. They stand in the harsh light of the streetlamps, and their moms comfort them before the show even starts.

One girl with braces and too much lip gloss seems particularly upset, almost like she's throwing a tantrum, and her mom is smoothing her hair and saying, "I know, sweetheart . . . I know . . ." over and over, which isn't helping at all. And I'm reminded of the teen idol tragedies I read about for my social studies extra-credit assignment—there's one where a girl actually got killed by stampeding fans at a New Kids on the Block concert in the nineties. For just a moment, I get a little nervous, wondering if that could that happen here—because of the crazy crying girls. If they ruin this experience for me, I swear to Gob, I will never get over it. Never. That's assuming, of course, that I live through it.

Just as the light turns green and we take our first steps into the crosswalk, a police car races by us with its lights on. It taps on the siren in a warning, and the crowd scrambles to jump back on the sidewalk and out of its way.

"What the hell?!" someone shouts.

"I can't believe he didn't kill someone!" shouts another.

My mom puts her arm around my shoulder and watches as the police car careens away from us. "That would really suck if you died right now, before you even laid eyes on Rory Calhoun," she says.

Eventually, we safely cross the street and fight our way through all the people—my mom holds my hand and leads with her right shoulder, pulling me behind her, saying, "Ope! Excuse me! Thanks. Excuse me! Thanks." It's a little bit scary, so I not only willingly hold her hand, I actually hold on tight, with both hands.

No one else seems to be moving in the same direction we are. Instead, we're fighting against a sea of completely stationary people. Nobody is going in. When we make it through the crowd, I look to the right, and I see people coming out of the Pop Tasty Bagel Bite Center. Security guards are holding the doors, and people are actually streaming *out* of the building instead of going in.

We find a ticket taker with no crowd in front of him, and my mom holds out her phone to show him our tickets—but he doesn't even look at them.

"I'm sorry, ma'am," he says, "but we're not letting anyone into the building at this time, as there's been an emergency that has caused the indefinite postponement of tonight's show."

"Wait . . . what did you say?"

"I'm sorry, ma'am, tonight's show has been indefinitely postponed due to an emergency. We're not letting people into the building. Your ticket vendor will contact you regarding a full refund if you wish."

"Oh my God—do you know what happened?" My mom reaches out to grab my arm protectively but keeps talking.

"No, ma'am, I don't."

"Are we in danger? Do we need to leave the area or something?" She grabs my arm tighter.

"No, ma'am. Everybody's safe. But it seems to be a medical emergency for an individual."

She loosens her grip but doesn't let go.

"Does it have something to do with that police car that just raced by?"

"I'm not sure. Who knows, but, you know, it's possible. They haven't told us much except that tonight's show is indefinitely postponed."

"So we can't even go in?"

"No, ma'am."

"But what if we just want a T-shirt?"

I now realize she's just asking questions to put off the inevitable. If she stops talking to this guy, she has to turn around and face reality.

Reality is me.

"No, ma'am. We're trying to clear the building to avoid any confusion."

"But what if we just want a T-shirt? I guess I already said that."

"I'm sorry, ma'am. Everyone inside the building is getting the same announcement, and they're being ushered out as we speak."

"But all these girls . . ." She looks around and now sees the crying for what it is.

Those girls weren't crying because of Rorymania; they were crying because Rory Calhoun was just ripped out of their hands. They can't go in, but they can't leave either. If they leave, their dreams die.

"I'm sorry, ma'am."

"Oh my God . . . okay . . ." She turns and looks at me for the first time. She turns back to ask him another question, but he's giving his speech to another mom in line.

"Okay," she says again, looking around nervously. I don't look at her. I don't say anything. A lump forms in my throat that keeps me from speaking.

"Well . . . oh, honey . . ." She looks at me briefly and then looks around again, as if she doesn't know what to do. "I guess . . . let's start walking back to the car."

Walking through the crowd feels a little like walking through a war zone. Now I see what I didn't really understand before—girls everywhere, throwing tantrums, looking ridiculous. Some are crying like babies, and some are begging and pleading—for what? Some are angry, yelling. And all of it is directed at the moms who bought their tickets and drove them here in the family vehicle.

I will not do that. I am not a baby. I am not a bratty child. I will not cry and wail in front of all these people.

But when we reach the corner, the light is red, and we stand there awkwardly with all the other stunned people. My mom puts her arm around my shoulder—and that's when I crumple. I curl into her body, and I bury my face in her shirt. I try not to make any sound. I try not to heave with sobs. But I cry hard, holding her to me tightly to muffle the sound.

chapter 34

It feels weird to just turn around and go home. So we stop at the Chili's on Highway 100 so we can just sit and scroll through our phones for news. There has to be more information out there besides "medical emergency" and "indefinitely postponed." In the car, I check Rory's Flutter feed and his website, but they both say nothing. The fan pages and forums are full of nothing but questions, tirades, and random guesses:

These things are always drug related.

WTF? Who cancels a concert with no advance warning? Totally unprofessional. #FormerRCfan

Did it ever occur to you that Rory Calhoun could be seriously ill or injured? For all we know, he could be dead. #RCfanforever

My mom is super pissed. We had to drive three hours to get here, and I doubt she'll drive me back if they reschedule.

How much you wanna bet that tomorrow morning we see a story about RC going to rehab?

Don't be stupid. Has there ever even been a pic of him partying? He's super clean.

Love you, Rory! #PrayersforRory

#PrayersforRory

#PrayersforRory

Right now, the lobby at Chili's is the most depressing place on the planet, festive and bright and loud, but it feels like going to Disneyland after your dog dies—all that happiness just makes you even sadder. There's a white woman—she must be the hostess—with blue eye shadow and fuchsia lips, who hands my mom a square buzzer thing, and we wait under a big yellow paper-mache sun. The hostess with blue eye shadow and fuchsia lips makes marks on the dry-erase map of restaurant tables in front of her. She has no idea what just happened to me. None of these people know. They run around under all the piñatas carrying hot plates of fajitas, completely oblivious to the tragedy that just happened out there in the world. It makes me feel lonely—and mad at them. And the piñatas are making me sad.

The buzzer in my mom's hand starts vibrating and flashing with red lights, telling us our table is ready. We are standing right next to the hostess stand, and my mom doesn't even need to extend her arm fully to give the buzzer back to her. Does fuchsia lips lady not know that the buzzer is totally unnecessary when we're standing this close to her? And that makes me feel sorry for her. Everything is so irritating right now, and sad. Everyone is so dumb.

We follow her swinging ponytail, walking past tables of people eating nachos, like they don't even care that the biggest night of my life has just been stolen from me.

"Here ya go!" The hostess motions for us to sit in the booth in front of her like she's revealing the new car we just won.

We scooch in, but we don't open our menus. Instead, my mom says, "Why don't you check Rory's site again?"

I tap, tap, tap, and the site loads. "Nothing . . . last updated at five forty-five tonight."

Just then I get a wisp of conversation from the booth behind me. My head jerks to the side so my ear faces them. A youngish woman's voice says, "Oh my God, I just got a text from Skylie. She says the concert was totally canceled."

Are they talking about Rory?

Another youngish woman's voice answers, a little nasally, like she has a cold. "What? Oh my God! Oh my God!"

"What is it?" my mom asks. I hold my hand up quickly to say, "Hold on!" and I keep listening.

"Ask her what the hell happened!" the nasal woman says.

"Seriously," says the other woman. I hear the clicking of each letter as she texts,

and then a ding.

"Okay, Skylie says she has no idea. They just got there, and they kicked them out and said something about a medical emergency. Oh my God, that's scary!"

"Okay, but maybe he just lost his voice or something," says nasally girl.

"Is that an emergency, though? I need another margarita. Where's our waitress?"

"You should get a mango one this time. It's so yummy."

I repeat the conversation to my mom in a whisper, and she actually seems excited. "Yes!" she says. "Maybe he just lost his voice! So then they could reschedule right away! And no one's going to rehab! That could totally be it, right?" She looks at me hopefully.

"I don't know," I say. "I don't know." I'm still a little shaken. I can't really think about things and answer questions. I'm more just listening and watching and feeling and wishing it wasn't happening.

I hear another ding. But this time it's coming from my phone. It's Shauna.

Shauna: What's happening?
Shauna: Where are u?
Shauna: What happened?
Me: Idk. At Chili's. Trying to find out.
Shauna: Did you even get in?
Me: No.
Shauna: Are you okay?
Me: Barely.

"How about local news?" my mom says. "Don't you think they would be reporting something by this time?"

I tap the name of our local news station into the search bar, and a picture of Rory's face pops up immediately. "Here," I say. "It's a video! Reported at eight thirty-four—that's, like, a minute ago." I tap the triangle on the screen to start the video, and a young Asian woman with a short haircut starts talking.

"Fans of pop star Rory Calhoun had a big disappointment tonight when they arrived at the Pop Tasty Bagel Bite Center for tonight's scheduled concert. Ticket holders were turned away at the door and told that a medical emergency had forced Rory Calhoun to indefinitely postpone tonight's concert at the last minute. Many reported seeing an ambulance and several police cars drive away from the Pop Tasty at accelerated speeds around 7:30 p.m. There's no confirmation about where that ambulance went or who it was carrying, but we do have reports from witnesses inside the Pop Tasty, one of whom said that they heard shouting coming from the direction of Calhoun's dressing room and one who saw Calhoun running out of one of the stage doors. These are somewhat conflicting reports, so we will stay on this story until we get some verifiable facts from concert officials. One thing we could verify is that ticket vendors will offer refunds to those who request one, even if the concert is rescheduled. This concert sold out quickly, so this is surely a difficult night for many adoring young fans. Stay tuned to the Channel 14 news team for updated reports on this situation. This is Diane Ho reporting outside the Pop Tasty Bagel Bite Center."

And now I'm scared.

That doesn't sound like he lost his voice.

I feel warm and look up at my mom just as our server arrives at our table, her perfume telling me that she's standing right next to me. "Hi! I'm Marissa! Welcome to Chili's! Can I start you off with some specialty margaritas or our house-made lemonade?"

My mom holds her hand up toward Marissa, as if to say, "Excuse me for just a sec," something she would normally never, ever do to waitstaff at a restaurant—so rude.

"Okay then!" says Marissa. "I'll come back in a few!"

My mom focuses on me. "So that doesn't sound like he lost his voice," she says, looking concerned. "But it also sounds like it may not be Rory." I think she's trying to prepare me and make me feel better at the same time. "It could also be completely wrong," she adds. "They even said the only thing they can verify is that tickets will be refunded. Let's place our order and keep checking in."

I don't know if I can eat, but I look at my menu anyway. Now that I know there was an ambulance involved, I have a little bit of butterflies in my stomach.

"You know," my mom says, "it could even be someone in his crew. Or his band. Right?"

This time, I'm the voice of reason. "I don't think they'd cancel the whole concert if the lighting guy got sick."

"Well . . ." She's considering that idea. "But what if there was no lighting? That's a really big part of the concert. That really might ruin it," she says hopefully.

"He probably has an assistant or something that would just do it."

"Oh," she says. "That's probably true."

When Marissa comes back, we order nachos, and my mom does, in fact, order a mango margarita. When she says she would like a mango margarita, Marissa corrects her: "You mean a Mad about Mango Margarita?"

"Yes. That one," my mom answers, refusing to say it.

When our order arrives, we eat carefully, with caution, as if sudden movements or enjoying ourselves might knock this precarious situation off its axis and cause something really bad to happen to Rory . . . or us . . . or whoever.

Finally, at 10:45 p.m., we notice that no one is eating nachos anymore. We are the only ones left in the restaurant except for people stacking menus and mopping floors. We can't stay here anymore. And for some reason, that feels bad.

It's time to go home and admit that tonight happened.

In the car on the way home, we are quiet. "Honey, I'm so sorry."

"I know," is all I can say. I don't look at her. I just look out the window. The headlights coming at me are blinding, but I don't look away. I see how long I can stare at them before closing my eyes.

"I mean, I'm sad that this happened to you." Her voice tightens a little. "I know how important this was. I'm just . . . I'm just so sorry." She reaches over and puts her hand on my leg, letting it rest there in place of a hug.

I'm still just staring out the window. Saying anything more seems like too much work.

I check my phone one more time before going to bed— nothing. Even poor Diane Ho isn't updating anymore. I slip between the sheets and press my face into my pillow, pushing my feelings as far down as I can so I can find sleep instead of sorrow.

In the middle of the night, my phone pings.

I open my eyes and see that the screen is lighting up my bedside table. Quickly, I reach for it and knock my book, my clock, and an empty cup to the ground.

@rorycalhoun
My sincerest apologies to the people of Minneapolis. I'm okay. But still need your help. Will explain in the morning.

He's alive!

chapter 35

"*Millie . . . are you awake?* Millie?" My mom nudges my shoulder gently.

"Hmm?" I open one eye and look at the clock. It says 5:45 a.m.

"Millie? Are you awake? It's not him. It's his mom."

"What?" I keep trying to open my eyes, but I can only do one at a time.

"It's his mom. Rory Calhoun's mom is in the hospital."

"What happened?"

"It's on right now; I paused it. They thought she was having a heart attack or something."

I get up and follow my mom in her fluffy robe down the stairs and into the kitchen. She picks up the remote off the island and points it at the tiny TV above the sink, the one she uses to watch the news when she's making dinner. It's Diane Ho again. Poor Diane Ho—I bet she's been up all night.

". . . it's been confirmed that Rory Calhoun's mother, Maureen, was rushed to Northwestern Hospital at approximately seven twenty-five last night, just prior to her son's concert, which was to begin at eight. It appeared she was suffering from a heart attack, but since that time, it has been confirmed that that was *not* the cause of her collapse.

No further information has been provided to media sources except that she has been stabilized but remains in serious condition. I should add that Maureen Calhoun is only forty-three years old."

"See?" my mom whispers. She points the remote at the TV to turn the volume down again.

I feel relieved, and scared, and confused, and still sad—but relieved. I don't know how I feel, so I say nothing.

"Go back to bed, honey. You've still got an hour and a half to sleep. I just thought you'd want to know."

I stand there, still looking at the TV, saying nothing.

"Honey . . ." She gives me a soft hug, then pulls away and puts her hand on my cheek. "Go."

Instead, I look at her and ask, "Why are you up?"

"Couldn't sleep. I finally got up and started trolling for news. Apparently, TV news starts at four thirty in the morning. Please, go back to bed."

So I turn and shuffle away, just like all the other girls whose moms woke them up to calm their worst fear.

chapter 36

After I wake up, getting ready for school feels weird, like maybe they should cancel school. I know it's not like the president died or anything, but it kind of feels like that.

I grab clothes from my closet floor, not at all interested in planning something cute. My outfit from last night, the one I chose so carefully for the concert, is in a heap, and I try not to look at it. I try to pretend the heap is not there, essentially unused because Rory never saw them. I reach for a pair of leggings and a dirty sweatshirt just to the left of the heap. But my hand grazes the heap, sending a wave of mean coursing through my body, ending at my throat, which tightens up like I'm going to cry. Damn it! I kick the pile to the back of my closet and half cry, half whisper all of the worst words I can think of. "Mothertrucker!" Kick. "Stupid effing . . ." Kick. "Frank!" Kick. "*Frank!*" Kick. I kick and I kick at the heap, making sure it goes as far back in the closet as I can get it. Stupid outfit. And the tightness in my throat gets worse, and the words aren't helping, and eventually, the tears come. They pop out with a little sob, a quiet one. And I slink down to the floor and sit, hanging my head, surrounded by dirty laundry, and I say out loud the worst swear word I know, the one that has never once come out of my mouth.

Just like a kid who doesn't wash his hands after he poops. But I don't care.

After wiping my nose with a T-shirt, I go downstairs and put cereal in my bowl, but I don't eat it. I just look at it. I try to eat it, but I can't seem to swallow. I chew and chew and chew, but the sadness won't let me swallow. Eventually, I just spit it back in the bowl.

My mom walks in just as the chewed-up cereal tumbles off my tongue and into the milk. "Millie, sweetheart, are you okay?" She feels my forehead, even though she knows I'm not sick. She looks worried and pulls out the chair next to me and sits down.

"Do you want me to drive you to school?" She looks at me hard and smooths my hair behind my ear, grooming me and petting me at the same time. "I'm sorry, honey. It'll get better tonight, I promise," she says quietly.

I want to say thank you, but I can't speak. Instead I just keep looking at my cereal, all chewed up in my bowl.

I wonder if this is what depression feels like.

For a moment, I consider asking my mom if I can stay home—but she'll say no. Plus, I have a vocab and spelling test in language arts. Do you want to know what one of my spelling words is? Melancholy: m-e-l-a-n-c-h-o-l-y. Definition: a feeling of pensive sadness.

I stare at my cereal a little longer before dumping it down the garbage disposal. Why are food and sadness so incompatible?

In the mudroom, I pack my backpack without thinking, grabbing things close to me and throwing them in. Later, I will find Billy's *Hooty Owl* book, a box of tissues, one shoe, and a scented candle in there. Finally, I grab my phone and, just like I do every morning, I check Rory's Flutter feed before zipping it into the front pocket—nothing. It's like he doesn't even exist anymore.

I get to the end of the driveway when I hear my name.

"Millie!"

I turn around and see my mom coming out the door after me.

"Millie!" She still has her robe on, but she doesn't care. She runs down the driveway like she's running after her long-lost lover.

She slows just short of me and holds out her hand awkwardly. "Honey . . . you just left . . . you didn't say goodbye . . . or anything."

"I know, Mom. I just . . ." My words catch in my throat, and I look away.

She knows better than to hug me outside during bus time. Instead, she just reaches out and grabs my hand and squeezes it gently with both hands. "You just left—and I didn't get to wish you a happy birthday."

chapter 37

Your birthday should not be one of the most painful days of your life. I kind of wish I could skip it—or at least reschedule.

Plus, a middle school birthday is different. I don't bring a treat to school. I don't get a special crown to wear all day. It's like the first cruel gift of growing up—birthdays become less and less important with every year, until you're a grandma and you're like, "No, no, you don't have to do anything. I'm not really into birthdays." And you don't even want cake, because it has too many calories.

When I get to the bus stop, Joey McIntyre, Luke Perry, and Malik Zayne are the only ones there, all chasing each other. They do this thing where they tackle each other and try to remove one of the other people's shoes. Then they hold onto it until everyone gets to their lockers, so the shoeless person has to get on the bus, ride to school, and schlep to their locker with only one shoe on. They're so stupid. Malik runs by me, and his backpack slams into my arm. Today, this feels like a huge injustice. "Hey!" I shout after him. "Knock it off, you guys!" They ignore me and pull Joey to the ground, pulling his shoe off as he struggles. Idiots.

More people arrive, and it almost feels like an invasion of my space. I don't want to talk to anyone. I don't want to look at anyone. I just want to go home. Except for Joey and the shoe people, it seems quieter today. People, mostly girls, arrive and say nothing, looking down at the ground or off into the distance so they look occupied. They don't want to talk either.

When I see Shauna walking toward me, I get a lump in my throat again. Is this going to happen all day? I work hard to keep the lump right where it is so it doesn't turn into a squeak or something like crying. She arrives at my side, her thumbs hooked in the straps of her backpack, and gently nudges my shoulder with hers. And when the bus doors open, she drapes her arm around my shoulder so we can inch our way forward as one sad girl.

chapter 38

I walk into advisory and see that Ms. Peterman is wearing a T-shirt that says, "Cheer up, Sleepy Jean"—am I Sleepy Jean? Usually, I'm excited to see what Ms. Peterman is wearing; sometimes we spend the whole advisory talking about the sayings on her T-shirts. But today, it feels personal. And I look away.

I take my seat as she stands up and greets the class. "Good morning! Let's talk current events, people. Anything important happening this week that's setting the world on fire?"

I look down at my desk. I seriously can't do this.

Between classes, I check my phone. I check all his social media accounts, including Facebook, even though I know it's for moms. I check his official website and all the fan sites. They all say nothing. *Where are you, Rory?*

I check the Rory Calhoun Fan Club website and they keep posting the same thing:

As of this morning, there has been no information substantiating rumors of a heart attack suffered by Rory Calhoun's mom. There has also been no announcement regarding the sudden cancellation of his concert in Minneapolis last night. We will post updates as soon as they are available.

I feel the energy in the hallway behind me speeding up, as if the bell is going to ring. I keep scrolling, even though I know it will make me late. I don't care. For some reason, the threat of detention doesn't mean much to me right now. Last night's post said he would explain in the morning. It's no longer morning, and I'm starting to feel hopeless.

After lunch, I walk to my locker with Shauna. I tell her that this birthday is stupid and depressing and unfair, and I hate birthdays anyway, and I really seriously always have, and I might just forget about birthdays after this one because who really cares anyway? And she's nodding and saying things like, "Yeah, no one cares anymore." But she's smiling. It's weird. It sounds like she's listening to me, but it looks like she's mocking me. I don't think it's funny—at all.

That's when I arrive at my locker and find it covered in wrapping paper, bows, and pictures of whales.

"Shauna . . ." It's all I can think of to say. It's so beautiful.

"Did you seriously think I didn't care about your birthday?" she says, giving me a hug.

"When did you do this? How . . . ?"

"We had Drop Everything and Read time in the library today, and Darius let me sneak out. He gave me a note and everything."

"He let you out of library time so you could decorate my locker?" Apparently, it's not just Shauna—Darius, the library specialist, also cares about my birthday. I feel surprised and honored. And I really, really needed it.

"Did you see the acrostic I made?" She points to a sign with my name on it. "*M* is for Many talents (like collage and acrostic poems). *I* is for Irresistibly good conversationalist. *L* is for Loves her dog, Pringles. *L* is for Looks out for her friends. *I* is for Imagines a perfect world. And *E* is for Everyone should know and love Millie. And did you see this?"

She points to a photo taped up next to a postcard that says, "Whales of the Baja Peninsula." The photo shows two little girls wearing Brownie uniforms, standing side by side selling Girl Scout cookies in front of the hardware store. It's Shauna and me, on the day we met in second grade. I remember that day because some smiley white lady asked Shauna where she was from, and Shauna, super confused, said, "I'm from here." Then the smiley lady started talking about her pretty niece from Colombia. I had no idea where Colombia was, so I just pointed my thumb at Shauna and said, "She's from Laura Lane. It's just over there." We were so, so little.

"Do you like it?" she asks.

I stand by my locker with my face turning a little bit red, and I answer quietly, "Oh my God. Shauna . . . I can't believe it."

"And wait until you see this," she adds. She reaches out, grabs my lock, and expertly dials the combination. I'm not sure if I gave it to her or if she just watches me so often that she's memorized it. When my locker opens, there's a little stack of gifts sitting on the top shelf. There's a Twinkie, a tiny book called *Bulldog Friends*, and a small, framed photo, only a couple of inches high. It's so tiny that the photo is a little unclear. When I pick it up and hold it in my hand, I see that it's a picture of Rory Calhoun. He's walking on the beach, away from the camera, his hands in his pockets. His head is turned to look over his shoulder, straight into my eyes. To the right of his body is the word "Forever."

I hold it in my hand, feeling that combination of happy and sad that is so confusing.

Shauna pulls up close to me and looks at the photo over my shoulder. "Don't worry," she says quietly. "It doesn't have to be over."

Shauna is truly unbelievable.

I nudge her playfully in the ribs and put the picture in my pencil pouch so I can carry it with me. I want to thank her, but I'm a little choked up, so I just look at her and smile.

"You're welcome," she says, and takes a bow.

The halls get more crowded as we get closer to the bell. People pass by with backpacks and books, and they all glance in my direction to see the beautiful locker with whale pictures all over it. People I know say, "Happy birthday, Millie!" as they run by: Cassidy David and Randi Gibb, Amina Gale and Trinity Breen. Doni Ozmin and his sister, Marie, who I used to play with because our moms are friends, each give me a high five. Carson and Hawthorne stop and attempt to sing a totally made-up birthday song, so badly and so loudly that everyone in the hallway turns to look. People I don't know wish me a happy birthday too, which is funny and embarrassing but nice because I think they really mean it. Sad, boring Mr. Sneed calls, "Happy birthday, Millie!" from across the hall as he enters his room—even though I'm sure he cares nothing at all about birthdays. Even Scott Fenwick, the nice guy with the gentle brown eyes and tan face who gave me the note in social studies, says happy birthday as he passes by. This must be what it's like to be popular.

And it never would've happened without Shauna and her locker art.

It helps. It really helps. For just a moment, the happy feelings feel bigger than the sad feelings, and I don't really care how the rest of the day feels—because I had my birthday moment.

This time, when I check Rory's Flutter feed, I feel just a little bit less bereft (sad and lonely, especially through death or someone's departure).

chapter 39

My mom meets me at the door when I get off the bus after school. When I was little, she would meet me at the bus stop on my birthday with a present or a cupcake or something like that. But last year, she started meeting me at the door instead because she knows that a mom at the bus stop is babyish. I'm so proud that she understands this.

She hugs me and takes my backpack and hands me a small box. For some reason, the sadness lodges in my throat again. Maybe because my mom is trying to make me happy, or maybe because I'm worried that I won't like what she's giving me. Maybe because this tiny box is definitely not a toy and might be a more grown-up or serious gift that you would give an almost woman instead of a little girl. I don't know.

I try to mask the sadness with a "What is it?" kind of smile and take the box from her hand. I untie the ribbon, lift the lid, and peel back the lavender tissue paper.

Inside is a delicate bracelet with a small charm in the shape of a whale.

"It's a charm bracelet," she says. "You collect charms from all the places you visit, until the bracelet is full of memories."

I try so hard not to cry. I went the whole school day without crying, and it was so hard, but I did it. I clench my teeth and I blink hard, but in the end, my face crumples, and the tears leak out, and my hands leap up to cover it all up.

It's so beautiful, and it's so wrong. The whole thing just breaks my heart because apparently, my mom is listening and paying attention, and she cares about what I love, and she woke me up to watch the news this morning, and she knows I'm not a baby anymore—and in return, I lie to her about whales. I'm tricking her about my whole obsession. She doesn't know it's not real. And right now, this gift makes me feel like such a bad person.

"It's okay," she says. She pulls my face into her shoulder and wraps her arms around me. "I get it. This is not an easy birthday for you."

I'm not sure she truly gets it—she can't know that I was faking about the whales—but whatever it is she's giving me in that hug, it's working and I take it. And I swear, I will find it in my heart to love whales for real from now on.

After my yearly birthday dinner of tater tots and chocolate milkshakes, Cheryl brings my cake to the table and sets it down in front of me. Last week, the two of us pored over pictures on the *National Geographic* website and chose an image to be transferred onto the top of my birthday cake—a whale tail springing out of the ocean and spraying shiny droplets of water into the air. I can see the green hills of what I am hoping is Bodega Bay in the background. It is so beautiful that I actually consider not eating it. I stare at it for a moment and pretend there's a tiny person sitting on those green hills, watching the whale. I imagine it's Rory Calhoun saying, "Happy birthday, Millie," and winking at me from far away.

Cheryl carefully places candles around the edges of the cake so we don't ruin the picture. And I think about my wish as she lights them. I know this probably doesn't work, but I always do it anyway. What if birthday wishes really do come true sometimes?

So just in case, I close my eyes. And I concentrate on these carefully chosen words: *I wish for the pain of last night to go away. I wish for Rory Calhoun's mom to be okay. And I wish for just one more chance.*

I open my eyes, blow out the candles, and everyone claps. We take our cake into the living room for the best part of my birthday, and it is not presents—seriously. I know that sounds crazy, but the truth is that the best part of my birthday is when my mom and dad tell the story of the day I was born.

They tell it the same way every year, and they look at each other and smile while they tell it, almost like remembering that day makes them totally in love with each other. Not in a gross way but in a very happy way, like they are meant to be together and they will never get divorced. And I feel like the day I was born made them that way. If you want to feel special and happy, just ask your mom and dad to tell you about the day you were born. Even if they aren't married anymore, I bet it's a happy story.

My birth story involves a fast food stop at Arby's on the way to the hospital, where my mom scream-cried, "I want my goddamn Horsey Sauce!' at a drive-through employee. Less than an hour later, I was born.

"A toast to Millie," Cheryl says as the story ends, and she raises her glass of milk in the air.

Mom, Dad, and Billy all raise their glasses too, and we clink. Then they each come over to hug me. "Happy birthday, Millie," my mom says into my ear. "I love you. Even more than my goddamn Horsey Sauce."

My dad says the same and squeezes me extra hard.

I roll my eyes like, *Okay, okay,* but I'm also smiling really hard because I love that story so much.

Billy gets in line to hug me behind my dad like it's a carnival ride or something. He clonks his big Darth Vader mask on my nose as he puts his arms around me, but he doesn't notice. He probably clonks a lot of stuff that he doesn't know about. "Happy birthday, Millie," he says, and pats me on the back like he's trying to be grown-up. Then he puts his tiny hands on my shoulders and shakes me back and forth, saying, "I love you! I love you! I love you!" in a strangled voice.

Cheryl reaches over and picks up my hand and squeezes it, then looks me straight in the eye and says, "That was a happy day, indeed."

For just a second, I forget about Rory Calhoun and my bad luck. There's a glimmer of happiness in my chest. It's almost like joy—just a little piece that pushes out the self-pity long enough to let me have a semi-decent, not-so-horrible birthday.

What happens next will go down in my personal history as the most important gift-opening moment of all time. My mom reaches behind her and grabs an envelope off the shelf. "And now," she says, "it's time for your big present."

I take the envelope out of her hand, and she looks at my dad and then Cheryl, and they all smile at each other like, *This is it!* I hold it in my hand and wonder what could be in the envelope. As you get older, more of your presents come in envelopes, and it gets harder and harder to tell what they could be. I savor the moment, watching my parents sit on the edges of their seats, waiting. "Is it big?" I ask.

"The biggest," says my mom.

"Mm-hmm," my dad says, winking at her.

"Christ on a bike, just open it! I'm dying over here!" Cheryl puts her hand on her chest like she's waiting for a heart attack.

Billy stands right in front of me, putting his hands all

over the envelope like he wants to help. My dad grabs him by the back of the shirt and gently pulls him backward to stand next to his chair. He affectionately wraps his arm around Billy's middle to make sure he stays put.

Finally, I put one finger under the flap and begin to tear.

"Okay, okay, wait!" my mom says, putting her hand over mine to stop the opening. "Let me just say that this gift is one of a kind. No other gift will ever be this big. Next year, you will probably get socks and underwear for your birthday. But we did it because we love you, and you're so smart, and you're so interesting, and we just want to honor that, so—"

"Yes, yes, she knows! Now open it! I can't stand it!" Cheryl says, laughing.

"And," my mom keeps going, "Cheryl is responsible for a lot of this. We owe her big-time."

"No, you don't. Nobody owes me a thing. You're my family, and I love you—now just open it."

I start to tear at the flap again, when my phone buzzes next to me on the table.

"Ignore it!" everyone says together.

I make a "Come on!" face that tells them I'm not stupid. Of course, I'm not going to pick up my phone during big-present time on my birthday. But unfortunately, my phone is close enough that my eyes wander over just a little bit and catch a glimpse, just enough for me to see that it's a notification from @fanclub_rorycalhoun.

I continue opening the envelope, but I take my time, hoping I can scan the notification, undetected, before I'm fully committed to exclaiming about my present and appearing adequately grateful.

"Wow, this must be good," I say, tearing a little more at the flap.

The first part of the post says:

Rory Calhoun cancels US tour due to mom's illness.

Oh no.

I pull out the card, and several folded pieces of paper fall out. My mom grabs them quickly. "Don't look at these until you read the card!"

The card has a whale on the front, very similar to the photo we found for my cake, with a tail flipping out of the water and green hills in the background. My phone buzzes again. I open the card and use the opportunity to glance over at the screen once more. This time it says @rorycalhoun.

Oh my God.

I read the message in parts so I look like my attention is focused on the present-opening ceremony. The first part of the post says:

So sorry to all my fans . . .

I look back to the card and start to read out loud. "Okay . . . Dear Millie, The more we learn about you, the more we love you. This year, we honor you with a gift that stretches your mind and fills your heart. And we get to go along too! Love, Mom, Dad, Billy, and Cheryl."

It's hard for me to hear my own words because my eyes are trying to take in two sources of information at once.

The second part of the post says:

My mom is really sick. She needs to go home right away.

Oh, poor Rory! Poor Rory's mom!

I try to grab the last part of the post while taking the folded pieces of paper coming toward me from my mom's outstretched hand; the post ends with these words:

And I need to go with her.

I unfold the papers slowly, trying to digest what I just secretly read on my phone. Rory is quitting. He's going home. And I start to wonder what that means for me, until the words "flight reservation" catch my eye.

"Oh my God," I say.

"I know!" My mom can hardly stand it.

The first piece of paper says "Flight reservations: Karl Jackson, Carrie Jackson, Millie Jackson, Billy Jackson, Cheryl Sundberg. Delta Airlines 1398 Minneapolis/St. Paul depart 5:03 p.m., arrive San Francisco 6:53 p.m."

"Oh my God," I say again.

"Look at the second piece of paper! Do you see where we're going?!"

A prickly feeling, like pins and needles, rushes down my body like a waterfall when I realize what's happening. The second piece of paper says, "Lodging Reservation: Jack's Cove, 24560 California Route 1, Bodega Bay, California, 94940. Waterfront Cottage, 5 guests."

I look back to the post. He says he's going home. Home is Bodega Bay.

Oh my God.

I cover my face with my hands because the tears are coming fast. I do that silent-cry thing into my hands, when it's like you're sobbing, but there's absolutely no noise coming out of your mouth.

I'm going to Bodega Bay, California. And so is Rory Calhoun.

"Oh, honey!" My mom comes over and throws her arms around me.

My dad comes over for a hug too. "Wow, I knew you'd be happy, but I had no idea you'd be this happy."

"Whales are really important to her, Karl," my mom says. "This could be like the beginning of her life's work. I understand, honey," she says into my neck while she smooths her hand over my hair to console me.

Cheryl comes over and throws her arms around all three of us and sings, "We're going to California! We're going to California!" And Billy jumps side to side, right, left, right, left, until his Darth Vader mask flips off his head and onto the floor, unmasking a face that is much more excited than Darth Vader could ever be.

I finally muster the ability to speak. "I'm going to Bodega Bay?" I ask through my tears.

"Yes, honey, you are."

"Like, now?"

"We leave this weekend."

"You're taking me out of school?"

"Just a couple days."

"Seriously?"

"Seriously."

"I can't believe it . . ."

I'm going to Rory Calhoun's home.

And so is he.

I will never not make a birthday wish—ever.

chapter 40

Dear RC,

My hand is still shaking as I write this. Yesterday my dreams were destroyed–and today they are coming true. I am going to Bodega Bay to visit the beautiful home of the only person I have ever loved. I wanted to do this to feel closer to you, to see where you went to school and where you surfed and where you ate barbecued oysters and where you played Yahtzee. I wanted to feel you in the place where you became you. I didn't even hope to see you there because most stars don't hang out in their homes much after they become famous; they're on tour or living in Los Angeles or New York, where they go on TV shows or make videos and stuff. I really didn't think this would be a Rory-finding experience. But . . . *but* . . . you are going home. Please let home be Bodega Bay . . .

Love and hope,
Millie

My phone pings twice in a row, and I put down my pen.

@fanclub_rorycalhoun
Rory Calhoun will break his silence and give a live interview on *Good Morning USA* tomorrow morning at 7:00 a.m.!

@rorycalhoun
My heart is full as I thank you all for your support. I'm so sorry to disappoint everyone, but my mom needs me. I will explain tomorrow on *Good Morning USA*, 7:00 a.m.

Me: U up?
Shauna: Yup. Did you open your big present?
Me: You won't believe it.
Shauna: Is it a pony?
Me: Bigger.
Shauna: Is it a mastodon?
Me: Stop it!
Shauna: Tell me!!!!!!
Me: My whole family is flying to Bodega Bay this weekend.

There's a pause.

Shauna: SHUT THE FRONT DOOR!
Me: I know. I'm in shock.
Shauna: One more time . . . SHUT THE FRONT DOOR!
Shauna: Waitwaitwait . . . did you see RC's last post?
Me: Yes . . .
Shauna: Omg . . . Millie.
Me: I can't even say it.
Shauna: Is this seriously happening?
Me: If it's not, please don't wake me up.
Shauna: Happy birthday, Millie. Happy Franking birthday. ☺

chapter 41

Good Morning USA
Channel 12
6:33 a.m.

Faith Franklin: Coming up in the next half hour, we'll be interviewing young pop star Rory Calhoun about the cancellation of his US tour and why he chose to make such an unprecedented move.

"Millie," my mom whispers in my ear. "Why don't you get up? Rory's on TV in just a few minutes."

When I come downstairs, she has moved the kitchen table over so we can see the little TV while we eat breakfast. Usually, the little TV is just visible to the people doing dishes and cooking at the stove.

6:59 a.m.
Faith Franklin: After this break, we'll be back with Rory Calhoun.

My mom reaches for the remote and turns up the volume. I put my spoon back in the cereal bowl and wait.

7:03 a.m.

Faith Franklin: *The world responded with confusion and sadness two nights ago when Rory Calhoun abruptly canceled his Minneapolis concert just thirty minutes before it was scheduled to start. Fans worried about the health and safety of the superstar, and rumors swirled around the Internet about a drug overdose and possible rehab. Subsequent reports revealed that it wasn't Calhoun but his mother, Maureen, who had collapsed backstage in a frightening episode that appeared to be a heart attack.*

Via satellite from Minneapolis where his mom is currently hospitalized, we'd like to welcome Rory Calhoun to the GMU studio. Rory, first let me say, on behalf of the GMU family, how sorry we are about your mother's illness.

Rory Calhoun: *Thank you, seriously. We need it. And can I also say thank you to my fans and everyone who has sent me encouraging messages? I've never needed it more. You guys truly saved me.*

Faith Franklin: *First off, can you tell us how your mom is doing?*

Rory: *She's stabilized, and she's resting. The doctors and nurses here in Minneapolis have been amazing and so respectful and so comforting, and we're really trying to get her well enough so she can travel and we can get her home. And she's close. Maybe by tomorrow.*

Faith Franklin: Can you tell us what happened, Rory? It's been confirmed that it wasn't a heart attack, but it was clearly something very serious.

Rory: Yes, it was. She suffered a severe panic attack, and she's been diagnosed with anxiety and panic disorder. Her feelings of anxiety grew until her body responded with symptoms of a heart attack. She felt extreme chest pain, disorientation, dizziness, and shortness of breath that caused her to lose consciousness. We all thought she was dying. And so did she.

Faith Franklin: So she's suffering from something psychological? It's not a physical disease that she's suffering from?

Rory: Well, yes, it's psychological in nature, but it's a form of mental illness. It's a disease just like any other; it just wasn't a heart attack. The physical symptoms she felt were actually happening. It's just that their cause was psychological rather than a disease or infection of the physical body.

Faith Franklin: Is this the first time your mom has suffered anything like this? Or was there a history of mental illness or psychological difficulty?

Rory: She's suffered from depression her whole life, but she was being treated with medication, and we thought it was working. Recently, things had gotten more difficult for her. It seemed like the medication wasn't working anymore, and she started suffering from more symptoms of anxiety. She was fearful a lot. She was afraid something bad was going to happen to me—she worried about stalkers and Internet trolls; crowds were becoming unmanageable. I think we were all just coping and trying to get to the next show with her in one piece, you know? I don't think any of us took this seriously enough; if we had slowed down enough to get her reevaluated, we might have gotten a new diagnosis and a treatment plan so she could've avoided this. I learned how important it is to fully understand how serious and dangerous mental illness can be.

Faith Franklin: *Do you think your lifestyle and your career contributed to your mom's worry?*

Rory: *That's the thing . . . it's not just worry, it's a disease. My mom is in the hospital. She's not okay. And yes, I can't help but feel responsible for what's happening to her. If we just lived a regular life in our own house in our small town, and she just went to work, and I just went to school without getting attacked by really well-meaning but kinda scary crowds . . . When your only son needs a bodyguard . . . what does that mean for someone like her? And yet she does it all for me.*

He brings a forefinger to the corner of his eye to wipe away the threat of a tear.

Rory: *Sorry.*

He looks down shyly and clears his throat.

Rory: *It makes me wonder if I shouldn't do this anymore.*

Faith Franklin: *Is that something you're considering?*

Rory: *Right now, I just need to get her home to her own house, where it's safe. She needs to recover and work on overcoming this disease. When that happens, hopefully I can continue to do what I love.*

Faith Franklin: *You've canceled nearly every performance in the foreseeable future—and what you've done is quite unheard of in this industry, outside of the actual inability to perform, say a throat complication or an illness. How did you make that decision?*

Rory: *You have to understand, I thought my mom was dying. I ruined the night of twenty-one thousand people the other night—but how many people would you be willing to disappoint if you thought the person you loved the most was dying? And although she wasn't having a heart attack, the truth is that depression and anxiety can be really dangerous. And I'm not going to let that happen.*

Faith Franklin: *There's a real possibility that this could end the short career of Rory Calhoun as we know it. Are you prepared for that?*

Rory: *I love what I do; it's a dream come true, and I'm grateful for it every day. But I love my mom more.*

My mom's hand goes to her chest when he says this. "Oh my God, that kid . . ." she says.

Faith Franklin (turning toward camera): We have more information about anxiety and panic disorder on the Good Morning USA website, including a link to NAMI, the National Alliance on Mental Illness, the nation's largest mental health organization, dedicated to bettering the lives of millions of Americans affected by mental illness.

The screen fades to black, and the phone number for the NAMI Helpline appears.

This time, I don't use the fan letter guidelines. I don't decorate. I just say what's in my heart and send it fast, in an email.

Dear Rory,

It is with great sadness and concern that I write you this email. You have been my favorite performer for a really long time, and I can't imagine liking anyone else more than I like you. That's why your sadness hurts me so much. Your sadness feels like my sadness. Your mom's illness is such a tragedy and so unfair—seriously unfair and cruel. I would do anything to make it go away.

I watched your announcement on TV, and it was very clear that you love your mom so much. Don't worry about the crying; many boys/guys/men don't know this, but showing your love for your mom and showing your heartache on TV with tears and such is actually a sign that you are a really good person. And this is why the world loves you. Yes, we think you're cute, and yes, we want to marry you, but the real truth is that we love you because you're funny and kind and clever . . . and you love your mom.

(But even so, please don't cut your hair. I love your hair.) :)

I don't really go to church, but I am going to pray for your mom anyway. I don't think God cares if I go to church or not. He's probably just glad I'm praying instead of breaking commandments and such. So I will do my best for you and truly pray with all my heart that this evil illness goes away forever and leaves your mom as beautiful as she was the day she gave birth to the one and only Rory Calhoun.

All my love,
Millie Jackson
(You may remember me from my fan letter decorated with bulldog stickers.)

I press send. And then I pray, with folded hands and everything. I close my eyes, and I say in my head, *Dear God or Jesus . . . please help Rory's mom. Please.*

chapter 42

FROM: rory@rorycalhoun.com
TO: millie.jackson@susanbanthony.k12.edu

Dear Millie,

Thanks so much for writing to me. My fans are super important to me, and it's because of caring people like you that I'm going to get through this difficult time. I'm not able to respond to each letter personally, and I'm sorry about that, but please know that this letter contains my heart and my soul even though it is seen by many people. Anyone who reads this letter has my heart for the moment.

I must ask for your forgiveness, as I struggled with the right thing to do about my concert tour; so many people saved their money and some drove long distances to see me, and I disappointed them. I do not take that lightly. But in my darkest moments, I worry that my mom is leaving this earth, and I cannot leave her side. I hope you understand.

I would also like to thank you from the bottom of my heart for the tremendous outpouring of support you've shown me and my mom. I've had thousands of posts, comments, and even letters, all of them beautiful and encouraging me to be strong. I read every single one and say a little thank you in my head to each and every person who takes the time to tell me they care. Your kind words mean more than you'll ever know. Every word helps and makes me feel like my mom's illness can be overcome. If we all work together, I think we can get a new understanding of anxiety and help each other so that we can end suffering like my mom's.

For right now, I embrace the opportunity to care for my mom in the home we love so much. And I hope the world will right itself soon so we can be together again.

Thank you again for your love and understanding. Please love your families and your friends today—you'll never know how much they mean to you until they try and leave you.

Love always,
Rory
P.S. I've attached a photo of Happy and me on the beach. I hope you like it!

I print both the letter and the picture and pack them in my carry-on.

chapter 43

We arrive at San Francisco International Airport during a record-breaking weather event in the middle of the night that keeps us in the air, circling for over an hour, waiting for the torrential downpour to go away so we don't miss the runway or skid sideways into a fiery grave. My dad smells like scotch because the passenger next to him got drunk and spilled his drink in his lap. Cheryl smells like french fries because her seatmates brought their Happy Meals on board and squirted ketchup on her slacks. Grandmas call their pants "slacks." I don't know why. And my mom smells like vomit because Billy threw up on the plane just before takeoff. Actually, the whole plane smells like vomit for the whole flight, thanks to us.

No one is happy to be here.

When we finally land, smelling like scotch, french fries, and vomit, we slog to the baggage claim area without speaking, where we wait for our luggage. Billy holds my mom's hand and clings to her leg, clutching his travel-size deodorant and burying his face in the shirt he vomited on. He must be so used to it that he doesn't even smell it anymore. The baggage carousel goes around empty for what feels like a year. No bags come out, no one leaves on their happy vacation, and we all just stand there staring at the chute, praying for a miracle.

Billy is the only one to speak, in a voice that carries across the baggage claim area, annoying everyone within earshot: "Mom, when will our suitcases come out?"

My mom doesn't answer.

"Mom, when will our suitcases come out?

She still doesn't answer.

"Mom, when will our suitcases come out?"

She can't ignore him anymore, because people are looking at her like, *Can you please do something about him?*

"Billy, how would I know that? How would I have any information about when our suitcases will come out?"

"Will it be soon?"

"I hope so."

"But when?"

"I don't know. We have to be patient."

"Like in the next five minutes?"

"Sure."

"So we'll go in five minutes?"

"Sure."

"Promise?"

"Oh my God. No. I can't promise that if I really don't know. I don't have that information, Billy. We just have to wait."

"You said it would be five minutes."

"Please stop talking."

There's a pause.

"How much longer now, Mom?"

A woman three people away from us says out loud, "Oh for Christ's sake!" and walks to the other side of the carousel to get away from us.

When the first bag appears at the top of the chute, the whole crowd lets out a sigh of relief and scrambles a few steps forward so they can be ready to get their stuff quickly and get the H out of there. People grab handles, yank bags, and stomp away in a cloud of frustration.

We drag our bags outside, where the rain falls in liquid bricks, not just wet but heavy and forceful, making us hunch and cover like we're dodging enemy fire. I swear, the rain actually hurts. It feels like it's slapping me in the face.

We wait on the curb for a shuttle bus to take us to the car rental lot. "A shuttle will arrive in approximately . . . five . . . minutes," says a canned voice on the loudspeaker. Which doesn't sound very long, but when you're standing there completely unprotected, getting slapped in the face by rain, it feels *really* long. And she's right, a shuttle does arrive in five minutes, but it drives past us without stopping.

"What the hell?" my dad says, rain sliding down his face.

The overhead lady says again, "A shuttle will arrive in approximately . . . five . . . minutes." Which is good, but a little more painful than the first five minutes. But guess what? That shuttle drives right by us too.

"Goddamn it!" My dad doesn't feel the need to get creative with his swear words. He also doesn't mutter this under his breath or anything. He says it on top of his breath where everyone can hear it, including people we don't know.

"A shuttle will arrive in approximately . . . five . . . minutes." Now she's just annoying. We also don't believe her anymore. And the next time we see a shuttle making its way toward us, my dad steps out into the road and holds his hands up like he's stopping traffic.

"Oh God, Karl, what are you doing?" My mom starts to run after him but then jumps back on the curb when a taxi honks at her. Which is probably good, because Billy's face is still buried in her vomit-y shirt, and he doesn't look like he's willing to let her go anytime soon.

Thank God the shuttle stops instead of running him

over, and my dad stands at the door shouting so he can be heard above the sound of the rain. The driver says something I can't understand, and then my dad turns to us and waves his arm like, *Come on!*—like it's a helicopter to safety, and the bad guys are coming soon. We grab our stuff and run, ducking from the rain, right in front of oncoming traffic, my mom dragging Billy like he's her third leg or something. And then it's clear why all the shuttles keep passing us—they're full. My dad shoves us inside anyway, and we squeeze into little pockets of space, straddling our suitcases, holding onto each other, trying not to lean on the door. "I'm sure this is illegal," says a woman seated nearby.

Cheryl turns and hisses back at her, "Kiss my ass, Donkey Kong."

My mom closes her eyes and blows out through her nose, pursing her lips. "Cheryl," she starts. But then she laughs just a little bit with her eyes still closed. The woman does a "How dare you!" look, and Cheryl looks out the window like she never said a word.

The shuttle drives for about, oh I don't know, *ten seconds* and then turns left into the car rental lot—meaning we could've walked here by ourselves the whole time. That hurts. The look on my dad's face when he realizes this goes from on edge to seriously over the edge, and I worry that he's going to swear publicly again. Which he does when he sees the line of people that wraps around the outside of the car rental office. This time he says the big one. The one that starts with an *F.* And he adds stuff to it to make it especially colorful and embarrassing.

We get in line, and we wait—in the rain. We all have our jackets pulled up over our heads, and Cheryl has a spare Target bag that she pulls over her head and down to her nose. She puts her glasses on over the bag to keep it in place.

By the time we get to our car, we are drenched and shivering with cold, like when you get out of the shower only to find that there are no clean towels—and you forgot to take your clothes off before you hopped in. My dad is stressed, big-time. He looks like he's grinding his back teeth into a fine powder when he pops the trunk and starts loading our stuff. Then we all silently find our places in the car and watch as my dad tests the wipers before he pulls out of the space. He turns it to fast, then faster, than fastest, but you still can't see anything out the windshield but rain.

He turns on the heat, and the smell of vomit fills the car.

"Listen to me," he says, turning around in his seat to look at all of us. "I don't know where I'm going. I can't see. I'm cold. And you all smell. So I don't want to hear a word out of anyone, not one word, until we pull into a parking spot in Bodega Bay, do you understand me? No chitchat, no questions, no music, no bleepity-bleep from the poker game on your phone." He looks at Cheryl, who puts her phone back in her purse. "If I don't have complete silence, we could end up in a ditch, or worse. We could careen off a cliff and dive straight into the Pacific Ocean, and that would really put a damper on my vacation. So everyone just sit quietly and let me do my job, okay?"

We look back at him in silence.

"Okay?!" he says again, irritated.

"Karl, you told them not to talk—"

"Just nod your heads!"

Which we do, even Cheryl. We nod our heads and slink down into the back seat, trying to be as invisible as possible so we don't die.

For hours, the wipers slap fast enough to start a fire, but they still can't keep up with the rain that slides down the glass like a waterfall. It's like driving underwater with the occasional glare of blinding headlights that make us all hold our hands up like shields. The road winds and turns, and I worry that we may be hugging the side of a cliff high above rocky shoreline, the kind of rocks that can kill you if your car somersaults over the edge. It's too dark and rainy to see if that's true, but I just feel like we're tilting a little bit, this way and that way, and why else would we be tilting? Oh my God, please don't let me die like this.

And sitting there in that silence, I feel the shame of what I've done. I've used a lie to drag my whole family halfway across the country, on an expensive airplane, to spend our vacation in this place that really isn't anyplace—it's just a random place on the map, with no Disneyland or Grand Canyon and not even a single waterslide in sight. We could be lying on a beach in the sunny, celebrity part of California, but instead we are perilously feeling our way in the dark to a random small town in the not-sunny, not-celebrity part of California.

All because of a crush I have on a guy that I've only seen in magazines and music videos?

Schmidt! I am a terrible person. And I hate California.

Just as my dad requested, the car is freakishly silent for the entire drive except for the roar of the rain and the constant slap of the windshield wipers. Finally, my dad makes a slow, sharp turn and brings the car to a stop. Oh thank God. And when my dad kills the engine, Cheryl is the first to speak.

"Cheese and bacon! This lady needs an outhouse!"

"Everybody just sit tight," my dad says, not looking at her. "Let's just get to our rooms and get to bed. You can use the bathroom then, Cheryl." It's still raining but just normal rain now, not "rip a Target bag off your head" rain. He steps out of the car and starts to jog toward the office when Cheryl rolls down her window.

"Karl! Karl!"

He comes running back, holding his hand above his eyes to shield them from the rain, and ducks down to her window.

"What?"

"I could really use a Mountain Dew," she says.

He clenches his teeth, stands up defiantly, and marches toward the office again, calling out to no one, "You can get your Mountain Dew tomorrow, Cheryl!"

I can't hear, see, or smell anything but rain as we drag our stuff out of the car, so I have no idea where we are or what it looks like. But as we walk to our rooms, it sounds like wood under my feet, like a dock or a boardwalk or something. I look up as my mom puts the key in the door, and, at close range, the place looks like a shack—not a cabana or a villa or a condo or any other vacation-type dwelling but a common shack. And a wave of guilt falls over me again. I will never get over this.

We drop all of our stuff on the floor of our room and walk straight toward our beds. My mom doesn't say a word about brushing teeth, even though most of the time she'd lead you to believe that you'll get cancer if you don't brush your teeth before bed. No one even speaks—just straight to bed.

I drop my clothes to the floor and climb in between the sheets in my underwear and T-shirt because I don't even have the energy to find pajamas in my suitcase. I pull the blankets to my chin and squeeze my eyes shut, shutting out this horrible thing that I've done to my family.

"I'm so sorry," I say as I drift off to sleep, not even aware that Rory Calhoun and I could be breathing the same air.

chapter 44

I sleep hard. And I dream. In my dream, I'm sitting on a plane that smells like french fries. I'm seated next to Rory Calhoun, but his face is fuzzed out, and I can't see it. But I know it's him, the way you know things in dreams. I keep trying to refocus my eyes so I can see his face. I'm straining, blinking, but nothing helps—he stays fuzzy. He looks right at me and he talks to me, but I can't understand the words he's saying because of his fuzzed-out face.

I'm also trying to talk to the flight attendant, who is mad because she can't get Pringles into the overhead compartment.

And just when I think I can't take it anymore, the sun wakes me up, poking me in the eye with a sharp ray of light.

I open just one eye and look around, blinking and focusing over and over, trying to get my eyes to adjust to both the light and the strange surroundings, remembering little by little where I am—Schmidt!—and how I got here—double Schmidt! I see that I'm lying on a pullout couch, dark brown leather on the arms, that sits in front of two unmade beds, fancy brass beds, kind of old-fashioned. There's a stuffed bird mounted on the wall. It looks like a tiny turkey. That seems weird. And there's a little kitchen with an old round table and a single counter with an antiquey-looking sink in it. There's a cereal bowl on the table with a spoon in it. I go back to the unmade beds—where is everyone? Did they leave me here all alone? Why would they do that? I don't even know where I am.

And then I hear voices, happy ones, outside the door. I get up fast, scanning the room for my suitcase. It's sitting in the middle of the room, unopened, like I dropped it and just kept walking toward the bed. I rip it open and start digging for a sweatshirt and some pants, taking things out and throwing them on the floor, wanting to be out there because those voices I hear don't sound mad or angry or wet or cold.

And as I stumble toward the door, shoving my arms in my sleeves, I catch a glimpse through the window . . . of steel-blue water and diamonds shimmering on its surface. I know that sounds silly and language artsy, but that is *exactly* what it looks like—diamonds. And what happens when you shine a bright, sunny light on those diamonds? They twinkle. I swear, it is so pretty and amazing that, for a second, I worry that it isn't real, like maybe this is still part of the Rory Calhoun fuzzy-face dream. I go to the window . . . and what I see makes all the worry and shame from last night disappear. The scene in front of me is not just pretty—it is amazing and unexpected and full of my family, in their pajamas, laughing and smiling, with warm cups of coffee in their hands, as if last night never happened.

I step outside onto the wooden deck I'd heard under my feet last night and see we are perched right over the water. I could jump from our room directly into the sparkly ocean below. I turn around and see that my hotel room is really a little red cottage perched on the edge of the ocean with a family of other equally adorable, brightly colored cottages. To the right, I see rolling hills carpeted in green grass. Are those sheep? Oh my God, I think those are cute sheepies grazing on the green carpeted hills.

Cheryl is in her nightie, leaning against the deck railing, staring at the twinkling diamonds with a shot glass full of Mountain Dew in her hand. She sees me and raises her glass, cheers-like, and says, "Good morning, sunshine." Then she reaches out and pulls me to her chest, wrapping her arms around me like I just fell off my trike. "Welcome to California, kid."

It feels so good, like she doesn't hate me or California.

We stand on the deck, her arm around me, and she points to the rocks and the surf just below us. My mom and dad are sitting on a big rock, snuggled together with coffee cups, not at all like married people but more like boyfriend and girlfriend. Billy runs back and forth on the sand, stopping occasionally to pick up pebbles and throw them in the water. He stops when he sees me and calls, "Millie! I saw a seal! A real one!"

I look at Cheryl in disbelief.

"It's true," she says. "On the other side of that rock is a beach full of seals. And this guy is the cutest little bugger you'll ever see. I think I'll put him in my suitcase and take him home with me. Oh my goodness, there he is!"

She points toward my parents' rock. I lean over the railing, and there, not thirty feet away from us, is a seal poking his brown, shiny head out of the water. It could be the cutest thing I've ever seen in my whole life. Billy and my mom and dad start chattering, "Hi! Hi! Hi, little guy! Hi, buddy! Come here, buddy! Come here! How are you?"

He snorts and shakes his head like he's going, "No, no, no, no, no, no, no . . ." and then dives back under the water.

Billy cups his hands around his mouth and whisper-shouts toward me, "It's a seal!"

Cheryl and I run down the steps and over to the sitting rocks for a better look—sheep *and* seals? This could be *better* than Disneyland.

The shiny head surfaces again, a little closer this time. "Is he playing a game with us, Dad?" Billy says.

"He must like you, Billy. You must be a good playmate."

"Who wouldn't like Billy? He's a charmer! He can even charm seals." Cheryl holds out her shot glass of Mountain Dew so he can take a sip.

The seal's black eyes look at me for a second, and then he sprays seawater out his nose before diving under a third time.

"Oh my God, I love him."

Did I just say that out loud?

"Let's call him Sealy," says Billy. All of Billy's stuffed animals are named the same way, with the animal's proper name plus a *y* at the end—Moosey, Cowy, Sheepy, Owly.

"Of course we'll call him Sealy, honey. What else would you call a seal?" My mom then turns and holds her cup out to me. "Wanna sip of my coffee?"

"Cream and sugar?"

"Lots."

I hold the warm cup in my hands, looking at the shiny seal swimming away, the sparkly water, the sheep on the rolling hills, my smiling family—and I take a tiny sip, smiling as it warms me up. It smells like my mom. And today it smells like happiness.

Dear RC,

Bodega Bay is the cutest, prettiest, quirkiest little place I've ever been. Is it exciting? No, it is not. There's no noise except ocean and seagulls. There's nothing to look at except nature. There's nothing to ride except waves.

But I love it! Isn't that weird?

Because I think you're here. I really do.

Before I came here, I told myself that I was coming to feel you, not find you. Because really, what are the chances of running into the world's most beloved celebrity while you're walking down the street? Even if it's his street? I assume they keep you locked up in unmarked cars and secret tunnels and stuff like that so you don't have to pose for pictures and sign autographs all day long. Instead, I only needed to see where you lived and breathed and grew and just "were" in order to feel like I had a truly everlasting Rory Calhoun experience.

But maybe finding you and feeling you are kind of the same. And when I say "feeling you," I mean I literally feel like the air around me contains pieces of you or something. Oh God, that sounds so weird! I'm not a weirdo! Please believe me! But this feeling, like your heart is beating near me, makes me look over my shoulder constantly, with a combination of hope and disbelief. Kind of like thinking, *Are you there?* and *Of course he's not there!* all at the same time.

It's not a bad feeling. It's awesome. I'm happy feeling pieces of you around me. Even if I never set eyes on you, this feeling will make the trip completely worthwhile.

Plus, there are bookstores and coffeehouses and oyster shacks, all places I know Rory Calhoun has been— I just know it. And there are surf shops. Apparently, there's a rule that you have to be completely crush-worthy if you want to work at a surf shop. I think my mom is considering surfing just because of the cute guys at the surf shop—my mom! The woman who said, "where's the seat belt?" when we went horseback riding last year. So that tells you how cute the surf shop guys are.

It's like Bodega Bay is full of good feelings. And even though I know I probably won't see you, I feel like I just might see you.

Love,
Millie

Shauna: Checking in with my bff. Where u at?
Me: Hola, mi amiga. California. Doy.
Shauna: Me knows that! Where u at RIGHT NOW?
Me: At Rory Calhoun's house.
Shauna: WHAT?!
Me: JK!
Shauna: You so mean. Guess what? I have good news.
Me: ?????????
Shauna: I got an email from my roommate at camp. She's part Filipino, and she has a white mom, and she doesn't know Tagalog either!!!
Me: NO! WAY! WHAT ARE THE CHANCES????? Wait, isn't the purpose of going to Tagalog camp to learn Tagalog? Why would you go to Tagalog camp if you already know Tagalog? I'm going to say Tagalog one more time. Tagalog.
Shauna: Yes, duh, but for some reason I thought I'd be the only clueless person. But not anymore! Me plus roommate will be clueless together! Much more excited about going now.

Me: SEEEE????? Camp hasn't even started, and you already have a clueless pen pal! I'm excited that you're excited.

Shauna: Thank you, friend. How is your trip?

Me: I love it here.

Shauna: Is it cool?

Me: No. It's pretty and happy.

Shauna: ??????

Me: I'm looking at sheep right now.

Shauna: What the Frank?

Me: No lie. Sheep hang out on these hills, and you drive right by them. They're super cute!

Shauna: Baaaaa.

Me: I want my own sheep.

Shauna: Can you bring one home for me?

Me: I'll put it in my carry-on.

Shauna: Will it make goat cheese?

Me: That makes no sense.

Shauna: I realize that now.

Shauna: Have fun. If you see RC, marry him.

Me: I'll send you wedding pix.

Shauna: You better. Over and out.

We drive the Pacific Coast Highway, which the cool people call the PCH. Every once in a while, my dad will pull over and say, "Look, kids . . . the Pacific Ocean." He says it every time. It's like he doesn't want us to forget what a big deal this is. And I'm not even annoyed or embarrassed, because I'm kind of saying it in my head at the same time.

We always get out when he pulls over. Sometimes we just stand by the car and stare quietly with our arms folded over our chests. Sometimes we run down to the beach for a quick visit. One time, Billy got too close to the crashing surf, and my mom freaked out, telling him how dangerous it was. He never took his eyes off the water and calmly said, "It's okay, Mama. Life would never harm us."

My dad's voice jolts me back to the car. "When are we going whale watching?" he asks. "We've been here two days, and nobody's said anything about whale watching, and I thought we were here because Millie loves whales so much."

And I totally forgot that I was supposed to like whales—oopsie.

chapter 45

This morning, my mom is on the phone researching whale-watching trips, and I wait on our deck, overlooking the water. I look down at the beach and see a boy hidden behind a hoodie, his hands in his pockets, head down, just strolling and occasionally looking out over the water.

I don't take my eyes off him until he is so far away that I can't see him anymore.

I'm sure that's not him. That's impossible, right?

I check Rory's Flutter:

@rorycalhoun
"The cure for anything is salt water: sweat, tears, or the sea."
—Isak Dinesen

@rorycalhoun
"Live in the sunshine, swim in the sea, drink the wild air."
—Ralph Waldo Emerson

@rorycalhoun
"There's no place like home."
—Dorothy Gale

Oh my God—he's here.

Dear RC,

I am trying so hard to stay calm. I knew I could feel you here, and today I tried to tell myself that it wasn't you walking on the beach, but I just have a feeling that I was wrong. Was that you, Rory Calhoun? Was that you in the flesh walking right in front of me? Oh God, I think it was you.

I watched you walk, and I thought to myself, *Whoever you are, I get you. I understand why you love this place. I understand why you walk by yourself on the beach.*

If I lived here, I would walk by myself on the beach every day too. And maybe we would run into each other. And then we would start walking together, side by side, every day.

I know why you needed to come home. I get it now.

Love and stuff,
Millie

chapter 46

I have to keep reminding myself that we are here because of my crush on whales.

The whale-watching boat is not exactly what I expected. I pictured something like a small cruise ship with cushy seats and a snack bar. But this one is more like a large fishing boat—it's small and cramped with no "inside" to speak of. There are no seats to speak of either, unless you're lucky enough to score a spot on the bleacher seat that rings the deck area. My mom starts to sweat when she sees the "railing," which is more like a loosely woven mesh curtain that hangs to the floor from a single rail. She reaches down and grabs Billy's hand and says sternly, "Listen to me, Billy . . . you will hold my hand the entire time, do you understand? You *must* hold Mama's hand. Don't let go of Mama's hand. Ever."

He looks at her, worried, and says, "You mean for my whole life?"

"No, Billy." I pat him on the head. "She means just for the boat ride."

"Oh." He relaxes and smiles at her. "Okay." He then rewraps his fingers around her palm a little more firmly, as if it's not such a bad suggestion, now that it's not for his whole life.

There's a kid who stares at me from across the boat. My mom chatted with his mom while we waited in line for tickets and found out they are on vacation too and that this kid is also in seventh grade. My mom made an "I can't believe it; this must be the craziest coincidence ever!" face, like maybe she thought I was the only seventh grader on the planet. So now I'm supposed to be best friends with him or engaged to him or something stupid just because we were born in the same year. I hate it when she does this, like every person my age is a potential playdate. The kid is a little round in the stomach, and he wears a black *Star Wars* T-shirt. When I look closer, I see that it actually says the words "Whitefish, Montana" in the shape of the *Star Wars* logo. I make sure to not let him catch me looking at his dumb T-shirt, and I avert my gaze out over the Pacific Ocean whenever I feel him staring at me.

I've practiced in my head how to be adequately excited for this whale-watching trip. It is not lost on me that this is the moment of truth, where my evil plan either bonds us together in happy family memories or reveals me as a selfish, deceptive, ungrateful drama queen. I promise myself I won't play the aloof teenager who's embarrassed to get excited about things (except when Whitefish, Montana gets too close). I will smile, and I will say, "This is amazing!" and I will even give Mom, Dad, and Cheryl a hug when it's over.

Because they did this for me.

All of this is for me.

As soon as we board, everyone circles the boat frantically looking for the best and most comfortable viewing area. It feels like a game of musical chairs, like we're all afraid the music will stop any minute, and we'll be the only one left without a chair. Which will actually be most of us because of the bleacher-seat situation.

There's a group of people clustered at the front of the boat with binoculars and walkie-talkies. Their jackets say "Sierra Club" on the front pocket. They have camping hats with drawstrings pulled tightly under their chins, and their eyes stay focused on the horizon. Already, without even leaving the dock, they site, point, discuss, and talk into the walkie-talkies.

My dad subtly nods his head in the direction of the Sierra Clubbers and whispers in my mom's ear, "I think they look official—they're the spotters." So we head toward the front of the boat and sandwich ourselves in among them.

"This is where the action is," my dad says to us. "If we can hang by these people, we'll be the first ones to know when a whale is spotted! It's like a front-row seat to the whale show!"

The engine revs, and Whitefish, Montana stumbles as the boat moves away from the dock. He frantically grabs the railing and then does this weird little dance move like he stumbled on purpose.

The guide says over the loudspeaker, "Hello, folks. Thanks so much for joining us today. I know you're excited to hit the road, so that's what we're doing, on our way to some of the best whale watching in the country. There are some gray whale pods feeding just north of here, so that's where we're headed today. If you want to see a tail fluke, or a tail flipping out of the water, you need to look for gray whales that are actively feeding. This is simple physics; all of the food is at the bottom of the ocean. In order to get to the bottom, a whale needs to dive deep. So just before they dive, they flip their tails high out of the water, which gives them more thrust to get to the bottom where the food is. I think you will agree that their enormous strength is truly impressive."

After all the pretend research I did on whales, I can't believe I never found that fun fact. That is actually very cool.

"It will take us a while to get to this feeding area," she continues. "So just sit tight and keep your eyes on the horizon. When a whale is spotted, I will make an announcement and tell you where to look using the face of a clock; if our boat was a clock, the bow in front would be twelve o'clock. So if I say whale spotted at three o'clock, you would look to the right side of the boat. Thanks again for riding with us today, and I hope you enjoy the show."

And then we wait.

The temperature drops as we forge ahead; everyone's shoulders are hunched up by their ears, the wind blows hair straight, and we get splashed with cold ocean spray. My feet hurt from standing already. I shift from foot to foot. Billy obediently holds my mom's hand. Whitefish, Montana is trying to look bored, but it's hard when your shoulders are hunched up by your ears—not that I was looking.

Finally, after what feels like hours of waiting, there's a flurry of activity. All the spotters rush together and point their binoculars in the same direction. The lead spotter says something into the walkie-talkie.

My dad leans down and excitedly whispers, "She just said possible sighting at one o'clock!"

We scramble and crowd in close behind the spotters. Cheryl even gives up her bleacher seat. All our heads turn toward the spot on the boat where the one would be, craning our necks, scanning. Then walkie-talkie spotter shouts, "Confirmed! Confirmed sighting at one o'clock!"

My dad lifts Billy up high so he can see better. "I don't see it!" he says in his worried little-boy voice.

"Look for the tail, Billy! Look for the tail!" my dad yells over the spray. Our eyes search hard for anything that looks like the biggest mammal on the planet. But all I see are waves.

Again, walkie-talkie spotter, louder this time: "Confirmed! Confirmed! Common loon at one o'clock! Repeat: common loon! Confirmed!"

"What?!" Cheryl says. "They're goddamn bird-watchers?"

My dad slowly puts Billy down, and we all go back to our places—except Cheryl. Her seat has already been taken by Whitefish, Montana's mom. She has a cardigan on her head for warmth, buttoned under her chin so her face is framed by the neckhole. She keeps trying to give Whitefish, Montana a jacket, but he won't take it.

"Freaky birders!" Cheryl says, holding tightly to the railing. "If a common loon makes them wet their pants, what will they do when they see a whale?"

An hour goes by. I can honestly say I have never felt this antsy in my whole life. It's a whole new level of antsy. It's like an antsy-ness that might kill me. I left my super lame phone in the car because there's no cell service out here and I didn't know I would need it for the excruciating boredom. I could be playing my Yahtzee app right now. And no one else will give me their phone, because they think I'm going to throw it in the water or something. This is torture.

I'm worried about Billy. I am a mature teenager, newly turned thirteen, with a healthy attention span, and I am losing my mind with cold, windy, uncomfortable boredom. He is a little boy who can't sit through a whole episode of *SpongeBob SquarePants*. If it's this hard for me, what must it be like for him? But then I see that he has busied himself with a loose button on his coat. I wish I had a loose button.

The guide interrupts my ennui—I asked my mom for another word for boredom because she said she didn't want to hear another word about boredom—and makes an announcement over the loudspeaker. "We're getting closer to the migratory area where the gray whales feed at this time of year. We're not sure if it's a pod of whales, but we'll head over there right away. Gray whales are known for being quite friendly, so they might even be happy to see us."

And finally, it happens.

I knew it would be big. And I knew it would be beautiful.

But I had no idea . . .

The moment we all lay eyes on the whale, every single person on the boat takes in a sharp breath in disbelief. I can hear it, like we are a chorus of surprised people.

A mother gray whale and her calf swim alongside our boat and shoot a stinky mist out of their blowholes. It's like a whale fart!

All the irritation and impatience from the last hour evaporate, and the boat erupts in amazement: we squeal and clap our hands like kindergartners. The whales swim with us, arching and diving for a good twenty minutes, and we keep squealing and clapping. It never gets old—never. We just keep squealing and clapping.

The whales put on a show, flipping their tails high in the air, over and over. It's like they meet under the water and tell each other, "Just flip your tail. They love that!"

And it's true!

A giant whale tail, dripping with water droplets and sliding back into the ocean, is just too amazing to get used to.

Billy's face is stretched into a shiny smile the whole time, and I feel like shouting, "Nature! Science! Happiness!"

because, seriously, it's like school, but so much better than school could *ever* hope to be. Nature is winning today.

I realize how relieved I am that I care about this.

I'm not just *pretending* to be excited. And I even think maybe I should be a marine biologist someday . . . and live in Bodega Bay . . . with Rory Calhoun.

I just planned my life.

During the boat ride back to shore, which is a lot faster and a lot warmer, my mom gives us pens and tiny pieces of scrap paper—pens and paper I refused on the outbound trip because it seemed childish—and Billy and I draw whale tails, over and over and over.

We sit on the narrow bleacher seat, and we perfect the image that is seared in our minds: two backs emerging above the surface of the ocean, one big and one small; a volcano-like blowhole; and hasty pencil stripes shooting out of the volcano, indicating the spray that was our first signal to squeal and clap. It is our new go-to drawing subject, a way to relive this happy memory again and again and again—forever.

chapter 47

After a long day of wildlife viewing, we decide to have a quiet movie night in our cottage, and we stop at a little country store on the way home to buy movie snacks. The store feels old-fashioned, with a screen door that slams and a counter where you can buy meat and sandwiches. It smells like ham and fresh bread inside. The paint is peeling on the wooden counter that holds the cash register—an actual old-timey register that shuffles and dings instead of an iPad you sign with your finger—and the shelves are packed with wine, T-shirts, postcards, and the most colorful fresh fruit I've ever seen in my whole life. It's like art, all displayed in pretty baskets. And, lucky for me, they have every kind of snack food you could ever want. They might even have Pibb. Maybe this is the store where Rory Calhoun found Pibb. And now it's his favorite soda.

"Oh look! They have Mr. Pibb!" my mom says.

"You like Pibb?!" I ask.

"Of course! Mr. Pibb is my favorite!"

"First of all, there's no 'Mister.' It's just Pibb. And why do I not know that?"

"Why did they take away the 'Mister'? That'd be like taking away the 'Doctor' and calling it 'Pepper.'"

"I have no idea. But, Mom, why didn't you tell me?!"

"Well . . . I don't know. I guess I didn't know it was so important to you."

She says we can each pick out our favorite junk food. Billy will probably mess up and buy a peach or something. And we all scatter, picking things up and bringing them to the counter where my mom waits with her Pibb and her wallet.

That's when he comes in the door, quietly and calmly so he won't be noticed. He catches the screen door with his hand and closes it casually, careful not to let it slam, like he's been here a thousand times and he knows that the door will slam loudly if he doesn't catch it. He wears the same hoodie as the boy who walks on the beach, faded orange, the hood up over his head. He keeps his head a little bit down as he walks the aisles, with his hands tucked in the front pocket of his sweatshirt, like he's worried that people might recognize his hands or something.

My feet stop right where they are, next to the cooler full of ice cream treats. My chest quivers a little, and I remind myself to breathe. If I stop breathing, I will fall down and die right here next to the ice cream treats. Breathe.

I watch as he moves toward my mom, who's looking at magazines, and he stands right next to her, doing the same. She reaches in front of him to grab a *TeenTalk*. I don't know why she's grabbing a *TeenTalk*.

And she says, "Excuse me, hon."

My mom just spoke to Rory Calhoun. She called him "hon."

And as she pulls her arm back, with the magazine in her hand, her body changes. It stiffens slightly. And even though you can't see that prickly feeling, I know she's feeling the same wave of prickles that surged through my body just a few moments ago. She turns her head slowly, painfully, to look at the face hiding in the hood, and when she sees it, her hand covers her mouth in disbelief. The whole thing happens in slow motion.

He holds her eye contact calmly, as if to say, "Yes, it's me; it's okay, please don't scream." Then he raises the index finger of his right hand and holds it to his lips. My mom nods her head, still in slow motion, telling him she will honor his request.

The men with cameras walk in the door less than a second later. They slam the screen door loudly, like they've never been here before, and stand ungraciously in the entrance, talking loudly and blocking the only exit. They say things like, "This sucks, man," and "Where the hell is this kid?" They laugh obnoxiously and put each other down and use the f-word, even though there are grandmas and children in the store; they don't even care.

And ironically, they don't seem to know he's here.

The three of us—me, my mom, and Rory—are frozen in place. We are the only ones who know what is happening right now: The door is blocked. He can't escape.

That's when my mom drapes her arm around Rory's shoulder and turns toward me. She calls my name. "Millie?" His eyes look worried and dart toward the door. "Will you grab your brother here some Cool Ranch Doritos? Your brother here wants some Cool Ranch Doritos, don't you, sweetheart?" He relaxes and nods his head without saying anything.

I'm still standing there, frozen, except now I'm thinking, *No, he doesn't. He doesn't like Cool Ranch. He likes Funyuns.*

"Millie?" my mom says gently. "For your brother?"

She stares at me like, *C'mon, Millie, you can do this.* The boy in the hoodie peeks at me from underneath his hood, just barely—just long enough to say *please*.

I feel that peek like a kiss on the cheek. The gaze of Rory

Calhoun landed on me, Millie Jackson, and I will never let it go. My hand opens at my side, completely involuntarily, like it wants to catch the gaze as it falls through the air, protect it, so I can hold it forever.

"Millie?" she says again, directing me with her eyes to look at the men with cameras—the paparazzi. My mom is trying to trick the paparazzi into thinking Rory Calhoun is my brother, so he can escape without being noticed. We are protecting him. We are Team Rory.

I run to the chip aisle and play my part. Cheryl and Billy and my dad have already chosen their snacks and placed them on the counter; now they are busy looking at postcards. They have no idea why I'm running up and down aisles, grabbing bags and delivering them to the counter with such urgency.

My mom's hand shakes slightly as she gives her credit card, paying for the snacks that are allowing the tween world's biggest crush to slip away undetected. As the men with the cameras move toward the beer aisle, I feel Rory slipping away, receding from our made-up scenario, little by little, and I'm going, *No, no, no—don't go!* and then, *Yes, yes, yes—go! Carefully! Go!* I'm still running, grabbing every cool-ranch-flavored item in the store for my "brother" hidden beneath the hoodie, but I'm careful to keep my eye on him. I drink him in as much as I can while he stands there by my mom. Her arm is casually draped around his shoulders as if he were her child. I absorb every cell of his hooded outline. And then, while he's looking at the beef jerky, I see him slip out the door.

And it's almost like he was never there. I knew that was the point of our game, for him to go away—*and we did it! Yay!*—but I am suddenly stunned and sad.

When the transaction is done, the snacks paid for, we stand there, my mom and me, sharing a moment of *Oh my*

God—what just happened? We hold our bags of Pringles and Bugles and Funyuns and lots and lots of Cool Ranch Doritos. We hold them carefully, like the world might fall off a cliff any minute. Why I had to hold a can of Pringles so carefully, I have no idea. And when we finally have the courage to look at each other, we are wide-eyed and silent, as if any sound or movement could still jeopardize our undercover mission or make the entire incident disappear from history. If I utter a single sound, a gurgle, a squeak, could my brush with real, in-the-flesh Rory Calhoun evaporate? The incident in which I stood next to him in real life, and my mom actually exchanged words with him and even *touched* him, putting her arm around his real shoulders—could it all disappear if I crunch this bag of Funyuns too loudly?

"What's wrong with you girls?" It's my dad. He has no idea what just happened. He's so dumb.

"Why are we standing here?" Cheryl doesn't know either. She's not dumb; she's just old.

Billy is too little to notice that we are standing there awkwardly, but he mimics Cheryl: "Why are we standing here?"

So we move toward the exit, Mom's and my shoulders touching as the screen door slams, and we take cautious steps out to the car. When we load our bags into the trunk, our hands finally free, my mom turns to me and wraps her arms snugly around me . . . holding on just long enough to say this really happened. She's not at all dumb.

Everyone else is already in the car, so we hesitantly do the same, letting go and finding our spots, not wanting to leave this place because this is where *it* happened. It's just the most important thing that has ever happened to me in my entire life—*ever.*

Until . . .

chapter 48

. . . this happened:

"Everybody buckled?"

My dad's usual pre-driving safety check is interrupted by a knock on the window.

Standing just inches away and separated by a thin sheet of annoying window glass is—I can barely say it—Rory Calhoun. He is back, and he's knocking on the window of our rental car and waving this adorable, tiny wave at us.

My brain is exploding, but there's a freaky silence in the car as my dad tries to open the window. He's pushing buttons and smiling at the boy, but the window won't go down.

Then my mom, very seriously but very quietly says, "Karl, open the window."

"I'm trying, Carrie, but . . . Darn it . . . What the heck?"

"Karl. *Open* . . . the window."

"Oh my God, Dad, open the window!"

"Open the window, Karl!" My mom is starting to panic.

The boy is still standing there. He's trying to help by pointing to buttons inside the car. *Please don't go*, I wish in my head. *Just please wait!*

Finally, my mom leaps over my dad's lap and starts slapping at buttons. "Open it! What's the problem? Just open the goddamn window!"

"Open the goddamn window, Dad!"

"Millie!" My mom looks at me in surprise. "We do *not* use language like that!"

"But you just said it!" How can she parent me at a time like this?

Argh! I can't stand it anymore! I launch myself over the front seat, and I slap at buttons with my mom, and suddenly Cheryl starts shouting, "Don't open it, Karl! He could be a carjacker!"

"What?!" That's three voices screaming, "What?" all at the same time.

"What are you *talking* about, Cheryl?" My mom stops slapping buttons momentarily so she can turn around and stare at her.

"He looks shady! Don't open it, Karl!"

"Oh, give me a break." My mom slaps my hand away so she can mash the same button. "He's a *child!* How can he be a carjacker?"

"He's wearing a *hoodie?!* The word comes from 'hoodlum'! Everyone knows that! Don't open it, Karl!"

"That's crazy! Every child in America is wearing a hoodie right now!"

"I'm not wearing a hoodie right now." Billy does not like to be left out of family discussions.

Slap, slap, mash, push . . .

Slap, slap, mash, push . . .

Finally, my dad turns the key, and my mom mashes a random button, sending the window down two inches.

Until I mash the button again—trying to make it go faster? I don't know!—and the window goes up.

Nooooooo!

Mash, mash, mash, two inches up, two inches down, up two, down two—poor Rory's head pokes in, pokes out, pokes in, pokes out.

"Millie! Just hold it down! Don't mash, mash, mash!"

"I can't help it! I'm nervous! Help me!" And then my mom gives me a hard shove, sending me to the back seat so I can't mash buttons anymore.

One final push, and the window slides all the way down, and we look out the window at our visitor like we are the calmest, sanest people on the planet.

My grandma takes in a sharp breath. "Millie! That's the boy on your wall!"

Oh my God, I can't take it.

He pokes his head in the window, and he just starts talking, like he's not even Rory Calhoun—like he's just a regular teenager, and we are just people he knows.

"Hey, guys, that was super cool. Honestly, you really saved me in there, and I super appreciate it—seriously. So I was wondering, if you're into it—and if you're not, totally no worries at all, you won't hurt my feelings or anything—but, if you're into it, I can get you tickets to a surprise show we're doing just for locals tonight. You know, like a thank-you sort of thing? It's at the biggest place we could find, over in Santa Rosa. I mean, if you're interested in that sort of thing. I don't want to assume that you even know who I am."

He gives a little laugh like he's sort of embarrassed, and we just stare at him in disbelief.

"I'm going to give you a phone number to call. Jane will hook you up." He gets his phone out and taps with his thumb. "Tell her you helped me out at the general store, and I'll send her a message so she's expecting your call. You know, if you want, no pressure. Don't feel obligated or anything, but it was just really cool of you to help me out. Oh yeah, you must know who I am, or why would you have even done something so far-out? So thank you—I really appreciate it. It's kind of sad, you know—I just want to hang out at home and stuff, but I have to be careful. I don't want to start a riot or something. The people here are pretty quiet, so they don't really appreciate stuff like that in their town, you know? So I do my best to keep it on the down low. But a guy has to get his Funyuns, right? Although I guess I didn't get my Funyuns. Well, that's all right." He waves his hand casually. "I can live one more day without Funyuns."

He just talks and talks like he's not even famous, and I just sit there, not saying a word, with my eyes locked on his beautiful face.

"Do you want our Funyuns?" my mom says.

"No! Oh my God, you don't have to do that!"

"Seriously! We can always go back and get Funyuns any time we want, so you should take ours! Karl, pop the trunk! Millie, get out and get the Funyuns!"

"Man, you guys are the best. Make sure to call Jane. She'll hook you up."

I jump out of the car and stumble to the open trunk. And Rory Calhoun, *my* Rory Calhoun, follows me—*me*, Millie Jackson. Rory Calhoun follows *me*. I ransack our bags until I find the Funyuns and then gingerly hold them out to him, like I'm handing him the baby Jesus or something. It feels like slow motion and warp speed at the same time.

When he takes them from me, our hands don't even touch, but I feel him anyway. Then he looks at me and smiles—and he says, "Thanks."

It's the smile from every poster on my wall. It's so beautiful, I almost feel like crying.

As he turns to leave, he holds his phone up and says, "Call Jane." And then he waves a little goodbye to me. All I can do is smile and nod.

And then he's gone.

"So who is this guy again?" my dad says through the car window.

"Karl! Don't be stupid!" My mom hits him on the shoulder. "It's like you've never been inside your own daughter's room. Or in our house for the last six months! What is wrong with you?!"

"Just kidding!" My dad smiles and does the handclaps from "Happy."

chapter 49

Jane emails us tickets, and the usher walks us all the way to the front row, right in front of the stage. To my right are steps onto the stage. And I immediately think, *What if he comes down here?!* I might cry before it even starts. All my dreams are coming true. Right now, today, I am getting everything I have ever wanted, and I'm only thirteen years old. If I never get anything, ever again, I won't even care.

When the lights start flashing and the drums start beating, my hands go to the top of my head, as if to keep it from exploding. My mom puts her arm tightly around my shoulder and starts jumping up and down, just like the hundreds of girls and moms that surround us so tightly. I didn't even know she liked him!

It's like riding a giant wave, a surge of power and sheer electric joy that could send us flying into shark-infested waters if we don't hold on tight.

With every song, the wave gets bigger, and the crowd gets louder, and my face starts to hurt because I'm smiling so hard, and I just can't stop, even if I look like a huge dork. I never take my eyes off him, not once. Not when the Rory Pack dances just a few feet in front of me, not when the girl behind me starts sobbing, not even when strobe lights spell out the words "Rory Loves You!" And not when he gets down on one knee right in front of me, winks, and says, "Hey there," into the mic.

Is he talking to me? I freeze, not wanting to assume but still not wanting to take my eyes off him.

"Can you tell everyone your name?" He holds the mic right in front of my face. He's definitely talking to me.

I lean forward. And I think I say, "Millie."

"Nice to officially meet you, Millie."

That means I said, "Millie"! Whew!

Still on one knee, he raises his face toward the audience and continues. "Millie's a good friend of mine, y'all. She's a stand-up person. Would you like to come up on stage with me?" He's looking down at me again, and the crowd screams, like they're excited for me and wanting to be me at the same time.

I blink and open my mouth, but nothing comes out.

My mom whispers, close to my ear, "Yes! Say yes, Millie!"

I squeak out a sound that must be yes, because he holds his hand out to me. Oh Lordy, I'm going to touch him. Oh God . . . I'm touching him. He guides me over to the stairs, and I walk, one step at a time, taking my eyes off of him for the first time so I don't fall down the stairs and end up on the news. They start playing the intro music to "Worldwide Crush."

And it absolutely crushes me. I am the "Worldwide Crush" girl.

A chair is waiting for me, and I sit down—again, carefully, feeling wobbly. I think he feels my wobbliness, because he never lets go of my hand, keeping me steady.

When he starts to sing, he takes my hand and holds it to his heart, the center of his chest, where his true feelings live. His hand is covering mine. I can actually feel his heart beating. I can feel Rory Calhoun's heart keeping him alive, beating underneath my fingers.

And at that moment, my heart breaks—for real. There's actually a pain in my chest. And I start to cry. Yes, I do. Just like all the other "Worldwide Crush" girls, I start to cry. My heart breaks, just like they sing about on the radio, just like my mom says when she talks about the day I was born. There's this mixture of happiness and joy that's so intense that it actually hurts . . . and it makes you cry.

And as I feel his heart beating in his chest with my own hand, it dawns on me that this fantasy won't end the way I want it to. It can't. It won't end with us getting married and raising bulldogs together by the ocean, because I'm in middle school—I just mastered long division, for Pete's sake—and he's a rock star touring the world.

And so I hold on. I take his hand, and I cradle it to my cheek. What I want to do is wrap my entire body around him like a human pretzel, my face in his neck, my arms and legs encircling him and making him a part of me. But I have just enough sanity to stick with the hand. I keep the hand.

And I don't let go.

I'm not sure how much time passes with me holding his hand. I don't even hear the song. Was it more than one song? I have no idea. But at some point, Rory wants his hand back.

But I'm not letting go.

He keeps singing and working our clasped hands into his movements, but it gets more awkward when I grab on with both hands, a little more desperate now. *Don't let him go!* my subconscious tells me. *Hold on tight! Once you let go, he's gone! Forever!*

When the song ends, he's supposed to move away from me and start the next song, but obviously, he can't. That's when I see a woman with a walkie-talkie on her belt climb the stairs to the stage. I know what she's for—she's here to end my fantasy.

Rory can't start his next song, so he starts talking to me and the audience. "Hey, everybody, I want to thank Millie so much for being on stage with me tonight. Can you say hi to the audience, Millie?"

I can't. Because I'm still crying. He holds the microphone to my mouth, but I just cry into it.

"Oh, it's okay. I know—it's a little overwhelming up here, isn't it? That's how I feel sometimes too."

The audience loves this and goes, "Awwwwww!"

The lady roadie with the walkie-talkie speaks sweetly to me, although I don't hear what she's saying, and eventually she gets me to loosen my grip on Rory's hand. She holds my hands and tries to get me to stand up, but I can't. I try to, but I swear, it's just not happening. My legs are shaking so badly that they can't support my weight. I'm like a rag doll in the lady roadie's arms. So she puts me back in the chair, and I see two more men with walkie-talkies come up the stairs toward me. Oh no—are they arresting me? Is this against the law?

The three roadies pick up my whole chair, with me in it, and walk me toward the wings of the stage. When I'm lifted and properly restrained, Rory moves his head toward mine and whispers, "It's gonna be okay—I promise."

It's gonna be okay. Rory told me so.

When we reach the wings, my mom runs over and helps me out of the chair, wrapping her arms around me like a preschooler who just fell off the slide. I stand up shakily, and I stay in her arms, holding on, crying for a different reason this time.

Because I ruined it.

Instead of seizing the moment, like I practiced, I fell apart, humiliated myself—just like everybody else.

"I know," she says quietly into my ear. "I know."

And I feel like she does.

With the roadies on one side and my mom on the other, everyone helps me to a room offstage so I can lie down. They set me down gently on a scratchy garage sale couch, where I curl up and hide my face, squeezing my eyes closed to shut out the horror of what I've just done.

"She just needs a little space and some quiet," someone says kindly. "It's okay . . . she's not the only one." They bring me water, a cool washcloth, and more water. They're working hard to make me feel better.

Finally, a woman's voice says, "All right, guys, let's leave them alone for a bit. Mom, call us if you need anything, okay? And we'd be happy to have a driver take you home if you need it."

They don't know that my home is three thousand miles away.

Then they take their walkie-talkies and close the door behind them. And the world gets quiet.

My mom stays close, not saying a word. I am unmoving, lifeless, curled into the corner of the scratchy couch with my eyes closed, like I'm sleeping or unconscious. I never sit up; I never even open my eyes. I can't bear to look at her. I don't know if I'll ever be able to look at anyone, ever again. Occasionally I feel her move in closer, checking on me. But I don't move.

After an eternity of stillness—I can't tell if it's been thirty minutes or thirty hours—I hear her fishing for her phone in her purse. Then a sad, soft "Hi, Karl . . ."

A door opens, and I feel her presence leave the room. I am alone.

With her gone, my heart cracks open, and I cry into the arm of the couch, suddenly conscious of smearing my wet face all over the upholstery. It's not just the humiliation of what I've done, it's so much more than that; it's a sad goodbye.

I'm saying goodbye to Rory Calhoun . . .

I just closed the door on everything I've been thinking about, dreaming about, hoping for; I had planned a life that begins here. But instead, it's over. My childhood dream ends here, on this couch.

He was never going to love me. What a stupid little child I am. Even if I hadn't cried like a snotty baby, my hope of him choosing me tonight was a fantasy. The world doesn't work like that; he's famous, and I'm thirteen. I can't even sit in a chair next to him without crying—how was I going to be his girlfriend? Instead of falling in love with me, he's probably afraid of me now—or worse. He could be laughing at me.

Harder and harder I cry, letting go of everything I've dreamed about for so long. Oh God, what will I do with my posters? The thought of throwing them in the garbage makes my throat tighten as I strangle a sob.

Do I even need a secret notebook?

Who, exactly, will I be now? The Millie that everyone knows has been destroyed . . . She was a hopeful, naive little kid. And I am both embarrassed by her and sad to let her go.

That's when I hear voices outside the door. They're muffled, but I think I hear "Is she okay?" And then a doorknob turns.

I smell him before I see him. Not a sweet, "fresh from the pages of *TeenTalk*" smell but a sweaty boy smell—a little dampness mixed with shoe leather. It's not a bad smell, just real. It catches me off guard, like maybe I thought he'd smell fresh, like spring rain or cool morning dew. But I know it's him. It's so unlikely and so unreal, but even without opening my eyes, I know it's him. I want it so badly *not* to be him because I'm so embarrassed. And in my fantasy, this is not how I pictured it.

So I keep my eyes closed, like a little kid who pretends to be asleep in the car so her mom will carry her into the house.

"Millie?"

The sound of his voice startles me. It's not in a song or on a screen. It's here, with me.

"Millie?" He says it again. And this time he touches me—lightly, with his open hand on the back of my shoulder. It's like electricity entering my body.

His kind hand, his mouth saying my name—the urge to sob lodges in my throat again. But I stay still, buried in the couch, waiting for the world to end.

"Aw, sweetie," he whispers. And then he places his lips lightly on my forehead.

Times freezes.

We are like a work of art, a famous statue . . .

The moment sears itself into my memory for all time.

His lips leave my forehead, he straightens up, and I hear his footsteps moving slowly toward the door—and my heart breaks in a million different ways.

My first crush, the first person I fell in love with even though he wasn't a real person, is walking away. Except that he was real—*is* real. He's more real than I ever knew. I feel him right now, left behind on my forehead. Maybe my feelings weren't so dumb—maybe they were just real. No, I'm not going to be his "Worldwide Crush," but does that mean this entire Rory Calhoun experience has to be thrown away?

Which is what would happen if I let him walk out that door.

I will have wasted all this time, all these feelings—so many acrostics, so many collages, too much scheming, and all that money from Cheryl for this trip to California. And thanks to him, I found whales and this beautiful place, and I'm having fun with my family in a way I never thought I would again. They've hardly bugged me at all! Even my mom!

It all meant something. And just because he can't love

me back doesn't mean he's not an adorable, good, and kind person; a dog lover; a person who loves his mom more than his million-dollar career. He's the kind of boy I would like to fall in love with for real someday.

I hear the doorknob turn . . .

I don't care that he can't love me back.

I don't need him to marry me.

That was never going to happen, and, truthfully, I always knew that.

I just didn't want it to be true . . .

"*Don't go!*"

I shout it before even opening my eyes. Sitting up slowly, I put my feet on the floor and feel the hard, speckled tile beneath me. The lights are bright, and my eyes have trouble adjusting; when I first see him, his face is covered up by dancing spots that shimmer and pop around his head. And for a minute, I panic and think it may not be him at all. Is it just a sweaty kid they sent in here to bring me more water? But my eyes adjust, and the spots go away.

And there he is.

"Hey . . ." He says it gently, so soft, like he's trying not to scare me.

"Hey," is my brilliant reply.

He lets go of the doorknob and approaches me shyly.

"Are you okay?" he says, sitting down in a yellow plastic chair in front of me.

"Yeah," I say. "I mean, no . . . I don't know."

At this, we both laugh, and he reaches out to touch my cheek, cupping it like a concerned mom taking care of her feverish child. I'm aware that I might have nubby number signs imprinted on my cheek from the prickly upholstery. But I don't care. The gesture is like medicine, instantly making me feel better.

"I brought you some water," he says. "But it looks like I'm not the only one who thinks you're dehydrated." He points to three water bottles lined up on the floor next to my foot. "I guess when people don't feel well, we all think, *Oh no! Dehydration!*"

He smiles at his own joke, like he's trying to cheer me up. It feels good to laugh after so much crying. I look right at Rory Calhoun's face, just inches away from mine. On my posters, he doesn't know when our faces are this close. But now he's looking back at me, and he sees me. He knows my name. It doesn't feel like he's making fun of me. It doesn't feel like he would ever make fun of anyone.

I want to say something to him, something important. But I'm tongue-tied. And I cringe, recalling the event that sent me to this weird garage sale couch.

"I'm so sorry," I say.

"Sorry?" he says quickly, knitting his brows in concern. "Why? What for?"

"That was . . ." I wave my hand toward the stage. "This whole thing . . . I have *never* been more embarrassed than I am right now. I will never understand what happened to me out there." I don't tell him how I've been practicing for this moment for months, how I looked down on girls who did exactly what I did. "And I hope you don't go back to your tour bus and make fun of me, the girl who had to be carried offstage with snot running down her chin."

He smiles and kicks my toe lightly, like something a kid in my class would do. "Hey, it's okay. You got overwhelmed, that's all. You're a real human, aren't you?"

"Yeah, a real human who feels real stupid."

"Seriously, you're not stupid. It happens to a lot of people. You know, the first time I went on TV, I wouldn't let go of my mom's hand?" He leans forward in his chair, his elbows on his knees. "Seriously! I wanted my mommy! They had to shoot me from the neck up, and my mom crouched on the floor next to my chair with her hand in the air. Oh man. Don't tell that to anyone or I'm toast!" But he's not worried; he thinks it's funny. He searches my eyes, and I can tell that it makes him happy to make me feel better. I don't want him to go. But he will. He has to. The sweetness of his voice and the softness of his skin and the . . . God bless America, it may not be my dream come true, but it is very, very close. How do I make him stay? I came all this way, and I know this can't last forever, but I need to at least try.

I look at his hands holding the water bottle—so clean, so real. He wears a ring on his right hand. Feeling brave, I reach out and touch the light blue stone with my forefinger. "What is this?" I say.

He offers me his hand so I can get a closer look, and I gently place my hand under his, our palms touching, pretending to look at the ring—but very aware that I am holding his hand. I stare at the stone intently, holding on ever so gingerly.

"Is it special?" I say.

"I just like it." He shrugs. "It's an aquamarine, the birthstone for March, which is weird because my birthday is in August . . ."

August 26, I say to myself.

"But I think it reminds me of the ocean. I live by the ocean, and when I'm home, I go there every day. And I hadn't been home for so long . . ." He sighs. "Is that weird? Wearing someone else's birthstone because you're homesick?"

"Like birthstone fraud?" I say, still holding my hand under his. "No, you're fine. You might get attempted birthstone fraud, but how could they ever prove premeditation?"

That surprises him, and he laughs.

"Oh my God, you're funny!" he says. "Most of the people I meet just cry. I meet a lot of freaked-out people, and

I always wish I could see them long enough to see the real person come out."

That's what I want too—to see the real Rory Calhoun come out. And I think I just did.

We sit across from each other and smile. And I fear our time together is coming to an end. But there's one more thing I want to say.

"I'm sorry about your mom," I say carefully.

His eyes hold mine as his lips form a sad smile. "Thank you," he whispers, reaching out to give my knee a soft tap with his pointer finger, like his words aren't quite enough.

"She'll get better," I add. "How could she not, with everything you're doing for her? How many rock stars would stop their whole tour to take her home?"

"I don't know," he says, looking down at his hands. "But she had to go home. And I couldn't let her go alone. That's just . . . sad."

He leans back in his chair and runs his fingers through his hair. "I made a lot of people mad, though. A lot." Looking at me seriously, he says, "Tell me the truth—do you think the world will still know who I am when I come back?"

"I don't know," I say honestly. "Does it matter?"

He looks down and nods his head knowingly.

"Funny *and* smart," he says, smiling. "Millie, you will be quite a catch for someone someday."

Does he know I wanted *him* to be that someone? Of course he does. Maybe this is his way of helping me put that dream to bed.

That's when the yellow plastic chair and the hard tile floor and the scratchy garage sale couch and the bright lights all disappear. I'm no longer worried about it not being what I pictured . . . because it turns out to be pretty close to what I pictured. When it's time for him to go, he gives me a quick hug—quick but tight, with his cheek right up against my cheek. He takes the ring off his finger and says, "Here . . . why don't you take this?" He doesn't say why. He just shrugs a little sheepishly and puts it in my hand.

And then he's gone.

I stare at the door for a long time. I don't want to run after him or watch him walk away, like some desperate groupie, so I just stare at the door and picture him walking down the hall with his hands in his pockets, on his way to his tour bus and maybe his mom. I look around the room, trying to catalog this moment so I don't ever forget: yellow plastic chair, speckled tile, scratchy couch. Me and Rory Calhoun—for real.

chapter 50

The next day, I'm too stunned to talk. I pack my suitcase in silence. My mom and I explained everything the best we could last night after we got back in what felt like the middle of the night. And I told my story over and over, even the crying part, which didn't feel so bad anymore. Because, my God, who cares, when it made Rory Calhoun so real, standing in front of me? They listen, and they listen, and they smile, and they hug me, even Billy, and I'm pretty sure they actually got it. And then I fell asleep so hard, even though I thought I would never sleep again.

I'm dying to tell Shauna, but I'm almost afraid to speak the words because already it's starting to feel like something in my past. I don't want it to be something in my past—I want it to be my right now.

I stop packing and send her a text instead.

Me: On my way home. Can't wait to tell you what happened last night. You won't believe it.
Shauna: Did you get married?
Me: Almost.
Shauna: You funny. Tell me now.
Me: Too many words. I'll come over when I get home.

Shauna: Cool. Karly Sanders told me you have a new project in social studies. Due in two weeks.

Me: Turd.

Shauna: And Scott Fenwick says hi.

We drive to the airport, return the rental car, fly home, wait for our luggage, find our car in the parking garage, and head for home. And although we've been traveling the entire day, that drive to our house feels like it will never end. I'm tired, and I need my own space, and I feel like sticking my head out the window like a dog, just so I can be by myself for a minute.

But when I see the sign for Laura Lane, my heart tightens and, once again, I get a lump in my throat like I might cry. Because as soon as we pull into my driveway, this adventure is over; Rory Calhoun is long gone and singing to someone else. I'll go to school tomorrow and become part of a life that doesn't include him. With each mailbox we pass, I silently plead, *Please, no*. . .

We inch closer and closer to my house, losing him a little bit more every second, and just as we approach our driveway, the song on the radio changes. When the intro to "Worldwide Crush" fills the car, my dad slowly drives right past our driveway and continues down our street and around the block, keeping my California dream alive just a few minutes longer. No one says anything, not even Billy.

He pulls into the driveway just as the song ends. And as the car comes to a stop, Cheryl puts her hand on my knee and says quietly, "That was nice."

chapter 51

It's hard to get up for school the next day. I'm tired and overwhelmed and embarrassed and overjoyed, all at the same time. By this time, everyone has seen me on YouTube—they know I'm the "Worldwide Crush" girl. They also know that I humiliated myself spectacularly in front of millions of people, one of them being Rory Calhoun. It's like dropping your lunch tray, throwing up in gym, and peeing your pants, times ten. What they don't know is the part that came after—the part that really matters. I'm starting over with a brand-new story. The old Millie was nice, and fun. But it's okay to pat her on the head and send her on her way. I'm not just Millie Jackson from Walnut Grove Estates and bus 2, the girl with the silly crush—I'm Millie Jackson, collage artist, acrostic poet, and close personal friend of Rory Calhoun—funny *and* smart. And ready for something new.

It's too late to go to Shauna's when I get home from the airport, so I tell her the whole story on the bus. She stares at me wide-eyed and silent the whole time; this is very unlike Shauna. She is stunned speechless. And when I'm done, she takes my hand and closes her eyes, almost like she's praying. "Millie," she says, finally looking up. "Today, you are a woman."

I don't even care about the humiliation anymore; it slips away little by little, and all that's left are warm fuzzies and gratitude.

I float through each class with a secret smile on my face, carrying my story with me. Word travels quickly, and I enter each class to a stunned chorus of "Is it true?"

When I get to social studies, Dr. Marion greets me with her arms open wide, pulling me into a hug, something teachers never do. It feels good, like she's giving her seal of approval, locking it in so my story will never go away. I take my hug and make my way to my seat in the back of the room.

There's a note on my chair. It's folded in a triangle and it says, "MILLIE" in all caps.

I take it in my hand and examine it, looking for clues. It's not Karly's handwriting or Shauna's.

I sit down and anxiously but carefully unfold the note, glancing at the clock to see how much time I have before the bell rings.

Inside, it says, "How are you? Love, Scott (Fenwick) P.S. Don't say fine. ☺"

I hold the note in my hand and look over at Scott Fenwick, gingerly, with just one eye. He is looking at Dr. Marion while she begins our worksheet review, staring straight ahead so hard—too hard. He isn't blinking. He swallows hard, like he's nervous. Then he looks down for a minute, and his eyelashes brush the tops of his cheeks quickly. They're the longest eyelashes I've ever seen on a boy.

I'm not sure what I'm supposed to do. And I'm not certain what it means, but I feel like it means something. I study those ten words: "How are you? Love, Scott (Fenwick) P.S.

Don't say fine" and realize that Scott Fenwick has always been nice to me. He's always telling Theo to shut up when he says dumb stuff to me. And now I see that his hair . . . except for the style and the color and the length, is just like Rory Calhoun's. How did I not notice that before? For the first time ever, I dare to consider that someone, a very cute someone, might actually like me.

Is it possible that not all boys are idiots? I've been so annoyed with them for so long . . . but Rory Calhoun isn't an idiot. Maybe Scott isn't either. His face hovers above the pages of *Roll of Thunder, Hear My Cry*, his skin so beautiful, much too beautiful for a boy. It's smooth and tan and the tiniest bit freckly. It's not even summer, for Pete's sake. He just doesn't look like the kind of guy who would throw a dodgeball at my head.

That's when I decide: I'm tired of being worried. I just hung out with the world's most famous crush, and he laughed at my jokes and listened to what I had to say. He even asked me for career advice. If Rory Calhoun likes hanging out with me, why wouldn't this kid? And so, by some mathematical property, if Scott Fenwick doesn't like hanging out with me . . . I guess it just doesn't matter?

I flatten the note on my desk and write the words I would've been too scared to write before: "Okey dokey, artichoke-y. Love, Millie (Jackson)."

Okay, so maybe I don't know *what* to write—but I'm trying. I refold it into a triangle and toss it across the aisle. Theo, his tablemate, slaps his palm down on the note and absentmindedly slides it over to Scott. How did he know it was for Scott and not him? I pretend to read my book while Scott opens it . . . but I watch him out of the corner of my eye again.

He smiles while he reads, biting his lip like he's trying not to. His face turns a little bit red. And with just a few minutes left before the end of class, Theo's hand slides a reply back to me. I open it—and hold his words in my hands, knowing that seventh grade will be the biggest, scariest, saddest, happiest, and bravest year of my life so far: "What's your number, cucumber? Love, Scott (Fenwick)."

(cue music)

It started small,
Just a note and a smile,
That's all it takes to bloom.
And I've watched you grow,
So I know that you're ready.
Take a leap off the page,
I'll make sure that you're steady.
These arms are strong,
They'll hold you tight.
But my grip is firm, to give you flight.
Don't worry, girl.
Just a note and a smile . . .
. . . will change your heart for good.

—from "Just a Note and a Smile"
Music and lyrics by Rory Calhoun

The End

a note to the reader

Worldwide Crush was inspired by my own real-life first crush!

When I was a kid, I fell hard for a boy detective who visited me every Sunday night at 6:00 p.m. He solved mysteries with his brother in a small town called Bayport and sometimes cracked cases while singing irresistible pop songs. That boy detective was Shaun Cassidy, star of TV's *The Hardy Boys/Nancy Drew Mysteries,* who *simultaneously* sold millions of records and concert tickets singing directly into my 1970s tweenage heart. His face on my vinyl record cover was so beautiful, I had trouble looking away. I spent hours daydreaming a whole life for the two of us—mostly at the beach, with horses . . . and puppies. I was quite gifted at daydreaming.

Without him, there is no Rory Calhoun. There's no Millie. There's no *Worldwide Crush.* This "relationship" the two of us had is the well from which this story came. When I was writing *Worldwide Crush,* I had to go back in time and re-feel all those feelings so I could write as authentically as possible. I watched *The Hardy Boys* on YouTube. I listened to my old records over and over, just like I had in my childhood bedroom. And I stared at that beautiful face on the cover, to see if my heart would melt again (FYI, it did).

Because we live in the age of social media, I was able to follow my first crush and see who he is today. Just like me, Shaun grew up. He put away his polyester bell-bottoms, and today he's a respected writer and TV producer. The first time he responded to one of my comments on Instagram, my brain just about exploded; this would have been unfathomable to the 1970s version of me! And when he learned about the book I was writing, he graciously sent me a personal note, giving me encouragement and sharing his perspective as one of the biggest teen idols of all time. The words he wrote in that note were as important to me at age fifty as they would've been at age ten. I still cried. I still printed the note and pinned it to my bulletin board so I could look at it every day. Just like Millie, I couldn't believe it when he said my name. "Hi Kristin," he wrote. *Hi Kristin!* Can you even believe it?!

He told me how worried he was back then that he wouldn't live up to everyone's fantasy of what a perfect first boyfriend should be. *Shaun Cassidy, the global superstar, was nervous?* I thought. *Who knew?!* But then he realized it was okay to be flawed; he was still a kid himself and on his own path to learning about love. And the one thing he would never ever do was dismiss those kids who loved him so much. He would never be cynical about them or look down on them—because their hearts deserved respect. *My* heart deserved respect. He knew that our love for him was a launching pad for our future loves as adults. And he took that responsibility very seriously. I can see Rory Calhoun saying the same thing himself, can't you?

". . . by writing your book," Shaun wrote, "you've not only honored them, you've honored our collective experience, and I'm so grateful for that. And so grateful for you. And I send you only love."

It's like a blessing for this book and all who read it.

Thanks for reading,
Kristin

guess what?

Hidden in this book are twenty-five references to celebrity crushes throughout all of crush history. Did you find them? Look carefully, because sometimes they're disguised! A boy's name might go to a girl. The name could be spelled differently or simply rhyme with the celeb name. Maybe the first and last names are switched around. Or it could be the name of a character they played on TV. You might need help from your moms, your aunties, your uncles, or even your grandmas because these crushes go *way* back. Go to kristinnilsenbooks.com to find out who they are!

acknowledgments

Anyone who's ever been to a movie with me knows I refuse to leave my seat until I've read the very last name at the bottom of the credits. Why? Because those people worked really hard—the gaffer, the Foley, the dolly grip, the dog trainer, the food service coordinator, even the guy who made the credits! How can you just walk out on that? I enjoyed a good movie, thanks to them! And so I sit and read until I'm the last person in the theater (while my family waits by the door, totally annoyed).

So in the spirit of moviemaking (don't go anywhere!), please allow me to roll the credits.

This book was made possible by many hands, including (drumroll, please):

Shaun Cassidy . . . because, duh. You were my first. And it left a mark.

Peta Gibb Weber, Andy Gibb's daughter and an important link to my personal crush history, who reached out and gave me a gift that validated how important this story was.

Anne Greenwood Brown, author of the *Lies Beneath* trilogy and many, many more young adult and adult books, who took me out to lunch to say, "I want you to write a novel." When I said, "But I don't write fiction," she very plainly told me to do it anyway . . . and I promptly found my calling.

Colleen Timimi, my first editor—and often my first reader, a fellow *Sally J. Freedman* fan who also has a seventh grader living in her head. And to Eva, who was my first IRL seventh-grade reader. Even though you are no longer in seventh grade, I will always look forward to your opinion.

Carolyn Cochrane, who wouldn't let me get on that plane by myself when my first crush announced his first concert since 1979. We traveled back in time together—you, me, *and* Shaun Cassidy—and all of that time travel made *Worldwide Crush* a better book.

Kathy and Colleen, who traveled with me to a tiny town in Northern California they'd never heard of so I could find a setting for my book. I will always be grateful for your patience as we stopped at every general store along the Pacific Coast Highway so I could visualize the end of *Worldwide Crush.*

Payal Doshi, Ellie Lippold-Johnson, Liza Gleason, Rachel Yenko-Martinka, Melissa Albay, and Betsy and Ellie Conway, whose feedback helped Shauna be as authentic and beautiful as she was in my head.

The Launch Ladies—Paola, Emilie, and Laura. Don't ever underestimate the power of bringing women together in a room to voice their deepest desires.

Tony and Kristin's beloved Grandma K, who was the first person to "ask the Google." Sometimes it takes just one phrase to inspire a whole book character.

Michelle Newman and Carolyn Cochrane, cohosts of the *Pop Culture Preservation Society* podcast, who did all the heavy lifting so I could birth this book baby. And then, *then*, they told the world about *Worldwide Crush* and gave me the stage for my first-ever reading.

Shane Martin, whose PR expertise was offered in a

warm blanket of support so I could reach out, in the most professional way possible, to *our* first crush. Yes, ours. It helps when your PR person has the same crush history as you.

Jennifer Cramer-Miller, memoirist and fellow She Writes Press author, who stayed up all night scrolling the Interwebs in service of a book *that was not even hers!* And in so doing, left a lasting impression on this book for all to see. Forever!

The students of Minneapolis's own Lake Harriet Community School. You were my laboratory while I wrote this book—checking out books, looking for yourselves in the pages, growing up before my very eyes. Susan B. Anthony Middle School looks an awful lot like Lake Harriet, doesn't it?

Jen Marie Hawkins, author of *The Language of Cherries*, who tried to edit this book but instead said, "It should just be published already."

Mary Cummings of Great River Literary, who believed me when I said I have a seventh grader living inside my head. The changes you made to this book are what the reader holds in their hands right now.

My queen, Judy Blume, who planted the seeds of this story in 1976 with *Tales of a Fourth Grade Nothing, Starring Sally J.*, and more. Thank you for the life-changing conversation we had, which you probably don't even remember. You'll never know how much it meant to me when you grabbed a pen and wrote "WORLDWIDE CRUSH" on that Post-it; that single act kept me from quitting.

The ModernWell Writing Studio—Nina, Julie, Amy, Katie, Betsy, Beth, Julie Jo, Carolyn, Melissa, Michelle, Kathleen, Colleen, Lindsay, Jennifer, and Heather—you are my incubator, my support group, my cheerleaders, my sisters in the trenches. These people, more than anyone, know what it took to make this happen.

The She Writes and SparkPress family for bringing my hard work to the world with precision and commitment. You people are seriously dialed, and I can't thank you enough for that.

All the grown-up people who shared their childhood crush stories with me at My Celebrity Crush Story. From fan letters and meet-cute fantasies to stealing kisses at the auto show, it all served as research and inspiration for the book you hold in your hands.

Gordy and Linda, for letting me put that hairy poster of Andy Gibb on my wall.

My husband, who doesn't complain about all the things I don't do (cook, clean, pull weeds, come to bed at a reasonable hour) because I'm probably busy writing. If Shaun Cassidy wasn't going to happen (like I totally thought it would), I'm glad it was you.

And Liam, whose genuine purity of heart makes me work harder every day. And whose philosophical questioning as a preschooler taught me how to write humor. Like "When bad guys die in jail, do they just throw them in the trash?" That's comedy gold. You were a genius, and you didn't even know it.

Many thanks to *you*, the reader, for making it to the end of these acknowledgments! And for sharing your precious time with me.

about the author

Kristin Nilsen has been a children's librarian, a bookseller, a perfume seller, a horse-poop shoveler, a typist (on an actual typewriter), a storyteller, a seventh grader, and a mom to both humans and dogs. Today she is a self-proclaimed Pro Crushologist who talks about Gen X pop culture on the *Pop Culture Preservation Society* podcast. She lives in Minneapolis, Minnesota, one of the only big cities in the world where you can look out your window and see a lake, which she likes—a lot.

Author photo © Belen Fleming, Belu Photography

SELECTED TITLES FROM SPARKPRESS

SparkPress is an independent boutique publisher delivering high-quality, entertaining, and engaging content that enhances readers' lives, with a special focus on female-driven work. www.gosparkpress.com

My Big Heart-Shaped Fail, Cindy Callaghan. $12.95, 978-1-68463-161-2. In a desperate attempt to clear her conscience, Abby Gray lets five balloons float into the sky with her deepest secrets attached to them—only to have them end up strewn all over her middle school. This middle-grade twist on *To All The Boys I've Loved Before* is perfect for reluctant readers!

The Girl Who Ruined Christmas: A Tween Holiday Novella, Cindy Callaghan, $12.95, 978-1-68463-115-5. When a California girl gets stuck in upstate New York for the holiday season, a clean teen, sweetly romantic Christmas adventure perfect for fans of Netflix's *Dash & Lily* ensues.

Gobbledy: A Novel, Lis Anna-Langston, $16.95, 978-1-68463-067-7. Get ready to meet everyone's favorite alien in the attic. Ever since Dexter and Dougal's mom passed away, life has been different—but things take a whole new turn when a shooting star turns out to be a creature from outer space!

Caley Cross and the Hadeon Drop, J. S. Rosen, $16.95, 978-1-68463-053-0. When thirteen-year-old Caley Cross, an orphan with a dark power, is guided by a jumpsuit-wearing mole into another world—Erinath—she finds a place deeply rooted in nature where the people have animal-like powers and she is a Crown Princess—but she soon learns that the most powerful evil being in *any* world is waiting for her there.